The Roar of the Falls

My Journey with Kaya

by Emma Carlson Berne

 AmericanGirl®

Published by American Girl Publishing
Copyright © 2014 American Girl

Questions or comments? Call 1-800-845-0005,
visit **americangirl.com**, or write to Customer Service,
American Girl, 8400 Fairway Place, Middleton, WI 53562.

Printed in China
14 15 16 17 18 19 20 LEO 10 9 8 7 6 5 4 3 2 1

All American Girl marks, Beforever™, and Kaya®
are trademarks of American Girl.

Special thanks to Ann McCormack, Cultural Arts Coordinator, Nez Perce Tribe

Cover image by Michael Dwornik and Juliana Kolesova
Cover waterfall image by Dennis van de Water/Shutterstock.com

Cataloging-in-Publication Data available from the Library of Congress

*In memory of Kathy Carlson,
born 1922, a judo brown belt who
could perform a jackknife dive,
kill a rattlesnake with a shovel,
sew sequined dance costumes, and
tame squirrels and crows*

Beforever

Beforever is about making connections.
It's about exploring the past, finding your
place in the present, and thinking about the
possibilities your future can bring. And it's about
seeing the common thread that ties girls from
all times together. The inspiring characters you
will meet stand up for what they care about
most: Helping others. Protecting the earth.
Overcoming injustice. Through their courageous
stories, discover how staying true to your own
beliefs will help make your world better
today—and tomorrow.

A Journey Begins

This book is about Kaya, but it's also about a girl like you who travels back in time to Kaya's world of 1764. You, the reader, get to decide what happens in the story. The choices you make will lead to different journeys and new discoveries.

When you reach a page in this book that asks you to make a decision, choose carefully. The decisions you make will lead to different endings. (Hint: Use a pencil to check off your choices. That way, you'll never read the same story twice.)

Want to try another ending? Read the book again—and then again. Find out what happens to you and Kaya when you make different choices.

Before your journey ends, take a peek into the past, on page 184, to discover more about Kaya's time.

Kaya and her family are *Nimíipuu,* known today as Nez Perce Indians. They speak the Nez Perce language, so you'll see some Nez Perce words in this book. *Kaya* is short for the Nez Perce name *Kaya'aton'my',* which means "she who arranges rocks." You'll find the meanings and pronunciations of these and other Nez Perce words in the glossary on page 186.

The Roar of the Falls is set in 1764, before America became a country. The story takes place on the Columbia River between present-day Oregon and Washington.

I lift my baseball cap and run my arm across my dirt-stained forehead. A thin Oregon drizzle falls from the steel-gray sky. Sitting back on my heels, I look around the raggedy garden plot. Actually, "garden" isn't quite right. It's an untidy patch of dirt strewn with rakes, trowels, wilting plants, mashed seed packets—and my team.

I can't help comparing this mess to my own garden. At home, I plant everything in straight rows with borders of marigolds to keep away the aphids. Dad and I made a fence this year, too, so now the rabbits won't eat my lettuce. I wish I could transport myself there right now, where it's neat and peaceful and I'm happy watching things grow.

Instead, I'm here—and right now, *this* garden feels like the last place I want to be.

I'm in this group of four girls for our end-of-year class project. We're starting a community garden for the food bank here in town. Neighborhood volunteers are going to tend it over the summer, after school ends. I was excited about the idea until Ms. Wallace assigned me to be the leader. I think she chose me because I know a lot about gardening already. It can't be

because of my leadership skills. I don't have any! I'm not into group things or clubs too much, and I'm not bold enough to talk to people I don't know very well. I've always been more of a loner—except for my best friend, Lily. Maybe it's because I'm an only child.

The project isn't going very well. Rachel and Sarah are just sitting together and whispering by the fence. I tried to tell them earlier to put up the pea stakes, but the long poles are still lying on the ground beside them.

Rachel sees me looking at her. "What?" she asks, narrowing her eyes. I swallow and pretend to be gathering empty seed packets. I don't say anything back—I'm not sure *what* to say.

On the other side of the patch, Greta has her earbuds in her ears and is singing along to her MP3 player as she pokes tomato seedlings into the ground. But the holes she's dug are way too shallow. The plants will fall out. And she's too close to the fence. The tomatoes won't get enough sun. I go over to her and take a deep breath. "Um, Greta?" I try. She doesn't hear me. I clear my throat. "Greta?" I say louder.

She looks up and smiles. "Yeah?" She pulls one

earbud from her ear.

"Um . . ." I hesitate. "D-don't you think those holes are kind of close to the fence?"

Greta looks down the uneven row behind her and tilts her head. "Not really," she says cheerily and pops the earbud back into her ear. She trowels up another shallow hole.

"Oh. Okay," I say to her back. Slowly, I walk over to the garden gate, a steady band of misery tightening around my chest. How can I do this? The garden is a mess. No one's working together, and at this rate, we're not going to have much to contribute to the food bank. We're going to fail the project, and it'll be my fault. I don't know how to lead this group.

◈ *Turn to page 4.*

Ms. Wallace is making her way through the patchwork of garden plots, checking on the groups. She's approaching our garden now. I straighten up and swipe at my face.

She stops and casts her eye over our chaotic plot. "Doing okay over here?" she asks. Her brown eyes pin me with their gaze, but she speaks gently.

I want to ask her what I should do, but my throat knots up. The words won't come. I can't seem to tell her that I don't know how to talk to the rest of my team. Instead, I nod my head, pretending everything's fine.

Ms. Wallace studies me for a moment. "All right," she finally says. "But I'm here if you need help." She smiles at me and continues on to the next garden.

I grab a trowel and begin furiously digging holes for pepper plants. I should have asked for help. I should have at least said *something*. I place the roots of a plant carefully in one of the holes I've dug and cover it with dirt. The scent of the rich black soil fills my nose, and I watch an earthworm curl its way back underground. I exhale, and the tightness around my middle loosens a little. Even though I feel stressed, digging in the dirt relaxes me.

Greta is still working her way down the row of tomato plants. Behind her, the little seedlings are already falling out of their too-shallow holes. Some of the stems are broken.

I kneel down at the far end of Greta's row and quietly dig a tomato plant deeper into the soil. Rachel and Sarah are hanging over the fence now, talking to some girls in the neighboring plot. I hear a burst of giggles and look up. They lower their voices when they see me looking at them. I blush and look away.

I stare down at the soil-caked trowel in my hand. Lily wouldn't let this project scare her. She doesn't let anything scare her. Like camp, for instance. She wants me to go with her to a two-week sleepaway camp this summer. "Just try it," she said. "You need some more adventure in your life."

"Don't you think adventure is kind of overrated?" I asked her.

Lily rolled her eyes at me. Then she turned her laptop toward me and showed me the camp website. There were lots of photos of girls sitting happily outside tents. "We can sleep under the stars every night!" she crowed.

I want to hang out with Lily this summer, and my parents have already said I can go, but I'm not sure about sleeping in a tent. Working in the dirt during the day is one thing. But sleeping on it at night isn't my idea of fun. I'm not brave enough to swim where I can't see the bottom, and I'm too shy to enjoy those getting-to-know-you games we'll probably have to play in a big group. Still, there were a couple of pictures of girls doing crafts, which I love, especially string weaving and beading. There was even a pottery wheel, which I've always wanted to try.

I work another tomato plant into a deeper hole. Greta is lying on her back now in a patch of grass with her eyes closed. My trowel hits something hard. I spot a gleam in the dirt and pull out a dusty piece of what looks like some kind of shell. I glance at it and stick it in my pocket. Between this garden project and the camp dilemma, I don't think this summer is going to bring me the adventure I'm looking for.

"How did your garden project go today?" Mom asks that night as we're all in the backyard. I'm kneel-

ing among my carrot plants, plucking out tiny weeds
and talking to the vegetables that have just started
sprouting. Dad is pruning the rose trellis while Mom
collects the branches he clips. In the gathering shadows,
fireflies blink and the soft fragrance of a late-spring
night has just started to rise from the earth.

I look down at the rich brown dirt caking my
fingertips. "Not great," I finally say. I tell her and Dad
about the episode earlier today. "I love *my* garden. I
know how to make this work," I say, waving my hand
down the tidy rows of vegetables. "But I don't think I'm
a very good leader."

"I think you need to practice talking to people you
don't know very well," Mom tells me. "That's the only
way you'll get better." She waves a thorny twig at me.
"Stand up straight, look them right in the eye, and
speak clearly."

*Or just flap my arms and fly to the moon. Because that
option is just as likely to happen.* I pull out a tiny bud
of a carrot by accident and pat it back into the earth.
"Sorry," I whisper to the carrot.

"And you should type up a plan and distribute it
to the group." Mom swipes up another handful of

trimmings from the grass and dumps them into an old basket. "Maybe the group needs to see the whole project to understand how important these first few steps are."

Mom's ideas are good, but I feel overwhelmed. To calm myself, I take five long, slow breaths. Then I try to focus on my hands methodically pulling the weeds.

Dad sets down the clippers and comes over. He perches on the edge of an overturned bucket nearby. "Remember what happened when I tried to teach you to ride a bike?"

I roll my eyes but can't help smiling. He knows I love that old story. He twinkles his eyes at me, and I feel the panic begin to ebb away.

Dad leans forward. "You really wanted to ride a two-wheeler without training wheels, so every day, we went out and practiced. And you just couldn't get it. You crashed onto every lawn on our block."

"And finally, you promised me that if I could ride one block without falling, you'd buy me ice cream from the Dairy Whip," I say.

He nods. "You were so patient that summer. And all for ice cream! It took you two weeks. You were covered

in bruises, but you did it. Remember?"

I laugh. "And you took me right out that very minute and we got huge sundaes. And it was before dinner! I thought that was the most amazing part."

"That's when we started calling you 'Wheels,'" Mom reminds me. We all laugh.

"Once you put your mind to it, you'll figure out a way to work with these girls," Dad says. "There's a reason Ms. Wallace asked you to be a leader."

Mom nods her head in agreement. I wish I was as confident as Dad and Mom. And Ms. Wallace.

❖ *Turn to page 10.*

When we're done outside, I take a shower and pull on my favorite purple-striped pajamas and my mouse slippers. I pick up my dirty clothes to dump them in the laundry basket, and something falls out of the pocket of my jeans. It's the shell I found while I was digging.

I pick up the shell and examine it more closely. It's round, and about the size of a half-dollar coin. There are two small holes in the middle. I wipe off some of the dirt. Beautiful pearly colors show through—pink, purple, blue-green, all swirled together. It looks like the inside of an oyster shell.

I take the shell into my bathroom and carefully wash it with soap under the faucet and dry it with a towel. Now the colors shimmer more than ever. I turn it over in my fingers. Someone must have carved it into this round shape and drilled the holes in the center.

Back in my room, I dig out my jewelry-making box and pull out some thin hemp cord. I decide to make the shell into a bracelet. Slowly, I twine the cord through the shell and around the outside, weaving it into a zigzag. It's a new pattern, and I haven't quite gotten it yet. There's one bit of cord that doesn't want to fit in with the others. It keeps sticking out. Again and again, I smooth it down, focusing on nothing but my fingers and the fibers. I add some beads to either side of the shell. As I work, I can feel my mind emptying out. I don't even know how much time has passed. The stress of the garden project and my worries about camp seem to float away.

I listen idly to Dad practicing scales on his flute downstairs in the living room. The phone is ringing in Mom's study. I knot the last strands, clip them neatly, and then tie the bracelet on my wrist. The shell glows like a pearl. Admiring the colors, I trace a circle around the edge of the shell with one finger.

Suddenly, I'm spinning so fast that my room seems to be whirling around. Everything is dark. What's happening? Did the power go out? I try to move, but my arms and my body are pinned by the spinning.

Then the spinning stops, and I realize that I'm on the ground. I open my eyes. Bright sunlight makes me blink. My bedroom is gone, and I'm sprawled on a patch of damp grass somewhere outside.

❖ *Turn to page 12.*

I push myself up out of the damp grass and stand up slowly, dizzy from all the spinning. I can't quite believe what I see. A broad river rushes by, feeding a giant waterfall, bigger than any I've ever seen. The water crashes over black rocks and fills my ears with its roar. On both sides of the water, the grassy riverbanks are covered with hundreds of shelters. Some look like tepees, and others are huts in different shapes and sizes. They stretch as far down the river as I can see. Steep bluffs rise behind me. Footpaths meander up the sides of the bluffs, and at the top, I can see horses grazing on the flatlands.

I'm no longer wearing striped pajamas. Instead, I have on some kind of a brown animal-skin dress that's decorated with delicate white shells. Fringe hangs from the front and along the hem. Lace-up leather moccasins wrap around my feet and calves. There's a small woven pouch attached to the soft leather belt at my waist. I recognize only one thing: the shell bracelet on my wrist.

My heart is pounding in my chest. Where am I? What just happened? *Don't panic,* I tell myself. I close my eyes and take five long, slow breaths. When I open my eyes, I'm still next to the roaring river, but I feel a bit calmer. Wherever I am, I can't just stand here in the grass. My damp moccasins slide a bit as I make my way carefully along the riverbank. There's a steep drop to the water below, and I'm still a little dizzy.

I see people in the distance. Their clothes are like mine, and everyone has deep brown skin and dark hair, which they wear in two braids—even the boys. I realize that the people look like the pictures of American Indians I've seen in my school textbooks. *How is this possible?* I wonder, as a group of children run past with what look like toy bows and arrows. Am I—could I be—in another time?

The overpowering roar of the waterfall makes my head ache. I'm confused and my legs are weak. I stumble, going down to my knees. I've strayed too close to the steep edge. Suddenly, the ground gives way beneath me and I'm slipping down the riverbank. Desperately I cry out, clutching loose rocks and soil, sliding toward the crashing water below.

◈ *Turn to page 14.*

❖omeone catches my arm. "Hold my hand!" a voice cries. I look up to see a girl's face above me. She clutches my wrist and pulls, and I claw my way back up the bank. Panting, I collapse on the soft grass.

"Thank you," I gasp, pushing myself up to my knees. The girl takes my arm and helps me to my feet.

I stare at the girl in wonder. She looks about my age, with black braids that reach almost to her waist and dark almond-shaped eyes that sparkle. She wears an animal-skin dress too, with fringe like mine, and the same moccasins.

She's staring back at me with concern. "Your face and arms are scraped," she says. "You're covered in dirt, too. I'll help you get cleaned up. Where is your family's camp?"

"Camp?" I say tentatively.

The girl sweeps her arm over the clusters of shelters spread along the riverbank. "Your camp is with the rest of the *Nimíipuu*, isn't it?"

"*Nimíipuu*?" I ask. It seems as if I should know what that means, but I don't.

"Of course you're *Nimíipuu*—we speak the same

language." She looks at me curiously. "But we've never met," she continues.

"I—I don't really know what's happened," I stammer. It's impossible to think over the roar of the falls and the strange twist of events. I don't want to lie, but I don't think I should tell this girl that I was transported here from my bedroom. "I just—found myself here," I say truthfully.

The girl takes my arm. "You've been frightened by your fall. You're confused. Come to my camp with me. It's not far from here. My grandmother will know what to do." The girl's brow is knit with concern. "I'm Kaya," she adds.

"Kaya," I repeat, my voice filled with gratitude. "You saved my life!" I look down the crumbled section of riverbank to the crashing, foaming water below. My stomach flops over with a nauseating twist. "You could have fallen, too!"

Kaya cocks her head to one side. "*Nimíipuu* always look out for one another. That's what my grandmother says." She takes my hand and squeezes it. I can feel how strong she is.

I try not to look shocked. This girl just risked her

own life to help a total stranger, and now she's acting as if it's not that big a deal. Does this happen all the time around here? Do people just swoop in and pluck one another from danger?

The reality of my strange situation crashes over me once more. Where is my family? Where is my home? Where am I? I sink down onto a nearby rock, trying to sort out my swimming thoughts.

"Are you sick?" Kaya asks. "Perhaps you hit your head when you slipped. I could get Bear Blanket—she's a healer." She turns as if to run.

"No, wait." I reach out and catch Kaya's hand before she dashes off. "It's not my head. I—I—" What I really need is a chance to think for a moment alone. "Maybe just a drink of water."

Kaya pats my shoulder. "I'll get water. Rest here." She dashes down the path toward the shelters.

As she disappears, I slide off the rock and onto the ground on the other side, so that I'm shielded from the path. I need to be alone. I need to think. First I was in my bedroom. I was sitting on the bed. I had made this bracelet. I look down at my wrist. Right before this thing happened, I had just put it on. Then I was

touching the shell, just like this. I trace a circle around the rim of the shell with one finger, and suddenly I'm spun dizzily, whirling again, the world in blackness.

❖ *Turn to page 18.*

I land with a thump on something soft and fuzzy and open my eyes. I'm lying on the carpet in my bedroom, wearing my pajamas. My jewelry-making things are spread out by my bed, right where I left them. The roar of the falls is gone. Instead, I can hear my father practicing scales down in the living room. The phone is ringing in my mom's study. Everything is just as it was when I left. It even seems to be the same moment.

Have I been in another world? I know I was wearing an animal-skin dress. I met a girl named Kaya. But now I'm back in my own room, and no time has passed. I'm wearing my own clothes again, and there are no signs of scrapes on my arms or face.

I look down at the bracelet on my wrist. Whatever is happening, the bracelet's doing it. Well, *I'm* doing it. I sent myself to that other world when I rubbed the shell, and that's how I got home. I could do it again!

Kaya's flashing eyes and friendly smile swim up in front of me. I'm surprised to realize that I want to leave the comfortable familiarity of my room and get to know the girl who saved my life. Maybe this is the kind of adventure Lily was talking about. As long as Kaya's

there, I think it's an adventure I'll enjoy.

Excitement seizes me as I place my fingertip on the shell. Holding my breath, I trace a circle around its edge. Once again, the room spins around me. I close my eyes, and when I open them, I'm on the grass, sitting behind the big rock, wearing the same animal-skin dress and damp moccasins. I'm back! But I can get home—as long as I have this bracelet.

I stand up and take a few deep breaths to stop the dizziness. Kaya's running back up the path now, and I wave to her.

"Here is some water." She hands me some kind of stiff pouch filled with water. I'm waiting for a cup before I realize that Kaya is watching me expectantly. I guess I'm supposed to drink right out of the pouch. It's a bit bulky and awkward, but I manage to get a drink of the cold, sweet water.

"Do you feel any better?" Kaya asks.

"Yes, thank you," I say, handing her back the water pouch.

"Do you want to walk to my camp?" Kaya asks. "Or would you like to clean up first?"

My arms and hands are still a bit dirty from my

fall, and my dress is streaked with dirt in a few places.
I could just dust myself off as we walk, since I *am* eager
to see where Kaya lives. But maybe I should take some
time to clean up.

◈ *To clean up,*
   turn to page 26.

◈ *To go to Kaya's camp,*
   turn to page 29.

Listen to me," Bear Blanket says, her tone serious. "I have something to tell you." Kautsa and Kaya turn to the healer respectfully. I sit up on the mat. I can't imagine not obeying when a grown-up speaks like that, and apparently Kaya can't either, because her eyes are locked onto Bear Blanket's face.

"Last night, I had a dream. A stranger came to us, a young girl, who had traveled a long way. She was searching for something, but she did not yet know what she sought."

I gulp. Could that dream have been about me?

Bear Blanket goes on. "In my vision, this stranger told us she could not stay, but was only stopping on her journey. She had to continue on, but she could not do so without help from the *Nimíipuu*."

Kautsa nods and then gazes at me. Kaya leans over. "Bear Blanket's dreams are given to her so that she can guide the *Nimíipuu*," she whispers.

"What does it mean?" My voice quavers a little.

"I don't know yet," Kaya confesses. "But we'll help you, just as Bear Blanket said. You'll find what you're seeking. I know you will."

Bear Blanket stands, and so does Kautsa. "Stay still

until the medicine has dried," Bear Blanket says.

"Kaya, stay with your friend," Kautsa says as she holds the flap of the tepee open for Bear Blanket. "But let her rest."

"Aa-heh," Kaya agrees, checking the herbs on my arm and head. "Lie still a little longer," she says to me. "My sisters will be back soon, and then we can work with them."

Kaya says "work" as though something fun is about to happen. I can feel her excited anticipation as I settle back onto the sleeping mat.

❖ *Turn to page 39.*

The three of us hurry upstream from the falls to a small plain. There I see a long, large hut covered with straw mats. Kaya calls it a lodge—it's like a tepee but oblong and much, much bigger. Outside, huge fires are burning, filled with beds of rosy, shimmering coals. Slabs of deep pink salmon are staked over the coals. They've been roasting slowly for much of the day. Women move among the fires, removing the stakes and placing the cooked fish in large wooden bowls.

Kaya's face lights up with an excited smile, and she hurries a little faster. "We are in time to help serve the food," she says.

As we duck through the flaps into the airy lodge, I'm puzzled by Kaya's excitement. I'm never this eager when my mom asks me to help with dinner. But once we're inside, I see that this isn't an ordinary meal. There's a large crowd, and I stop for a moment to stare at the sight of so many people. Rows of mats have been spread down the center of the lodge. All the men and boys are standing in a line on one side of the mats, and all the women and girls are standing in a line on the other side.

Kautsa, Kaya, and I join the row of women and face the men. A tall man that Kaya murmurs is Pi-lah-ka, her grandfather, leads the group in a prayer, as some men beat drums beside him. "*Hun-ya-wat* made this earth. He made all living things on the earth, in the water, and in the sky. He made *Nimíipuu* and all peoples. He created food for all His creatures. We respect and give thanks for His creations." Pi-lah-ka's deep voice and the words he speaks give me chills.

I find my throat swelling with emotion as I look around at the bowed heads and serious faces of Kaya's people. This community has worked together for this food, and now they are sharing it together. I think about my garden group. This is the point of our project—to provide food to people who need it. If we could work together, we could celebrate a harvest the way Kaya's people are celebrating the salmon.

Kaya nudges me. "It's time to serve the food we've gathered," she whispers.

With the other women and girls, Kaya and I place bowls filled with roots and berries on the mats. After I carefully set my bowl down and step back, I watch the men and boys place bowls of roasted meat on the

mats. Then several women—including Kautsa— bring in the large wooden bowls of salmon. I can tell that they are honored to do this job. The meal reminds me of Thanksgiving at my house, when my grandparents and aunts and uncles and cousins all crowd into the dining room and *ooh* and *aah* at the turkey while Dad carves it. This meal seems to be just as important as Thanksgiving dinner.

❖ *Turn to page 144.*

hen I tell Kaya I'd like to clean up, she gives a slight nod of approval and leads me up the path, away from the shelters. At a little stream that branches off from the river, Kaya kneels and plunges her hand into the water. "This is a good place to wash," she says.

In the stream? Are there germs in there? Or snakes? Kaya seems unconcerned as she scrubs her hands in the water, so I gingerly kneel beside her. The sun-dappled stream makes a happy sound as it burbles over the rocks. I clean the dirt from my hands and underneath my fingernails, which are always a bit messy from gardening. From the corner of my eye I see Kaya cup her hands and scoop water onto her face. I do the same, but when I brush against the scrapes on my forehead, I can't help crying out.

Quickly, Kaya pulls a handful of grass from beside the stream and gently presses it to my forehead. "This will ease the sting, but you need medicine," she says. "Let's clean your dress and then go back to my camp." Kaya finds a stout stick and helps me scrape off the dirt. That's when she notices my bracelet. "It's like my hair ties," she exclaims, touching her braids.

An electric shiver runs through me. Under each ear, securing each of Kaya's braids, is a round shell with two holes through the middle. The shells are the exact size and shape of the shell in my bracelet, and they shimmer with the same pearly colors.

"It's pretty! That would make a good trade tonight," Kaya says, gesturing to my bracelet.

"Trade?" I ask.

Kaya looks startled. "At the festivities," she says, as though I should know what she means. "Remember? There will be feasting and drumming and dancing, as well as horse racing, games, and trading."

Kaya's words make me flash to the pow-wow I went to last summer in Wallowa with my parents. I remember the drumming and the stamping feet, the boys with elaborate feathered headdresses and the girls with dresses covered with metal cones that jingled as they moved. Mom told me that all the different tribes from the area come together to celebrate their heritage. One of the tribes is called Nez Perce, but Mom said that they used to be called *Nimíipuu*—the same name as Kaya's people!

I remember the girls who danced at the modern

pow-wow. They had braids, too, and they wore shells in their hair, just as Kaya does. I realize that those girls are from the same tribe as Kaya. Could they be related to Kaya?

"I remember the dancing," I say softly.

But Kaya hears me. "*Tawts,*" she says. "Once you see the festivities, the rest of your memory is sure to come back."

I'm not sure what to expect, but curiosity makes me hurry to keep up with Kaya, who has started back up the path.

❖ *Turn to page 34.*

Let's go to your camp," I say, wiping most of the dirt from my arms. Kaya turns me around, and as we head down the path toward the riverbank, I dust the dried dirt from my dress.

As we walk, a man in leather leggings rides by on a spotted horse. He nods a greeting to a woman leading another horse. This one is dragging something that looks like a sled made of long poles. Colorful bundles are heaped up on the sled.

I can't help staring. "Kaya, that horse is pulling such a big load."

Kaya nods. *"Aa-heh*, but the travois has been carefully packed and is well balanced."

Travois, I say to myself. I've never heard that word before. Something tells me that Kaya's world is going to be full of new discoveries.

At the riverbank, I stare again. This time it's at the huge shelters of poles lashed together and covered with straw mats. Each one is as tall as a one-story house. Inside, the shelters are lined with poles and racks that hold rows and rows of fish. The fish have been cleaned and neatly cut and hang in long pink strips.

Despite the strong winds, the smell of the fish is

overpowering. I try not to wrinkle my nose. I don't
want to offend Kaya. But she seems far from offended.
She's grinning at the sight of all the fish.

"So many salmon have given themselves to us
already this season," she says. "We had to build extra
drying racks to hang them all." Kaya has to shout to
be heard over the sound of the falls. "Kautsa says the
wind here at the falls is another gift from *Hun-ya-wat*.
It dries the salmon so quickly that we don't have to
build drying fires."

"Yes," I murmur, staring at the women and girls
who are working all around us. One group is kneeling
on a large mat cutting up silvery fish. I swallow hard
as a woman skillfully slits a salmon down the belly,
takes out the insides, and begins scraping off the
scales. Other women are hanging trimmed pieces on
the racks in one of the big drying shelters. A girl no
older than me lugs a large fish up from the river and
lays it on a mat. The fish is nearly as tall as she is! The
girl straightens up, wipes sweat from her forehead, and
then heads back down to the water. I'm amazed at how
hard everyone is working. No one is slacking off, the
way the girls in my garden group did.

"Does everyone help?" I ask Kaya.

Kaya ducks under one of the drying racks and quickly reties a piece of salmon that is about to fall. Then she nods. "The men and boys work hard fishing, and the women and girls work hard preparing the fish they catch. That way, all the *Nimíipuu* have food to eat. Together we celebrate the return of the salmon with feasting. The fresh fish is a gift after a winter of dried foods."

I'm speechless as Kaya leads me upstream, away from the water. I've never thought of celebrating food the way Kaya's people do.

❖ *Turn to page 34.*

Before Kaya can say anything, three men rush onto the platform. They reach over the edge, and suddenly they're pulling the first man to safety. I can hardly believe he didn't fall into the rushing water and get swept away down the river.

It takes me a moment to find my voice. "What happened?" I ask Kaya.

"The men have ropes around their waists to protect them if they lose their balance," she explains. "The ropes are tied to the rocks."

"The man's rope caught him?" I ask.

Kaya nods. She looks relieved that the man is safe. We watch silently as the man stands with the help of the others. That's when I see the rope around his waist. I look up and down the river at the men on the other platforms. They're all wearing ropes.

I never knew fishing could be so dangerous. I'm grateful that the man is safe. I'm grateful that the others are there now, helping him off the platform. I'm grateful that Kaya reached over the edge of the riverbank to help me when I didn't have a rope around my waist.

I shudder as I turn to look at Kaya. I feel as if

I should thank her again for saving me from falling. But her eyes tell me I don't have to. Instead, she puts a hand on my shoulder.

"Let's get these fish eggs back to Eetsa," Kaya says. "She'll be waiting."

❧ *Turn to page 74.*

The sound of the falls grows quieter as we walk away from the water. Kaya and I round a curve in the path, and suddenly we're on the edge of a bustling village. There are tepees everywhere. Most of them are a triangular shape with poles sticking from the top. They're covered with some kind of straw mat. Dogs lie on the ground between the tepees, tongues lolling in the warm sun. Little dark-haired children play together, shouting to one another and squealing with laughter. They carry toy horses made of sticks or dolls dressed in miniature dresses just like the ones Kaya and I are wearing. Women bend over outdoor fires or kneel in front of mats, working on baskets and weaving ropes. It's crowded, and everyone seems busy, but there's also excitement in the air.

We're far enough away from the falls that Kaya and I don't have to shout to hear each other. Just then a group of girls passes us, chattering to one another. I can't understand a word they're saying.

I'm confused. If I can understand Kaya, why can't I understand those girls? Then I see two men using some kind of sign language. "What are they doing?" I ask Kaya.

Kaya stops walking and looks at me. She's confused that I'm confused. "They're throwing words," she says as if I should know what this means. When I don't respond, Kaya continues, "That's how people communicate when they don't know one another's language. There are so many different bands here at Celilo Falls. If we don't speak the same language, we use the sign language that everyone understands." Kaya puts her hand to my forehead. "You must have hit your head very hard if you've forgotten this," she says with concern. "Come with me."

I follow Kaya. It's true that I don't know anything about throwing words, but I do know where Celilo Falls is—or where it was. We went on a field trip to the Dalles Dam near my house last year. The guide told us about Celilo Falls, the giant waterfalls that used to be there hundreds of years ago. The falls were American Indian fishing grounds, she said, and then the government built the dam in the 1950s and the falls flooded and disappeared. I remember standing on the walkway at the top of the giant dam and staring over the silvery flat water at the highway curving around the huge lake that is there now. I remember trying to

picture how it must have looked before the dam was built.

I turn and gaze at the massive crashing waterfall in the distance. There is no dam, no interstate highway, no lake. Now I'm certain that I've traveled through time. Something tells me that I've gone back much further than the 1950s!

Kaya leads me to a group of tepees upstream above the falls. As we approach, I see two women, one older than the other, kneeling on mats outside the entrance to one of the tepees. Beside them, a fire pit simmers with rosy coals. In the shade of the tepee, two little boys are sleeping. A dog lies on his side, his paws twitching in sleep. He raises his head as we approach. When he sees Kaya, he quickly gets to his feet and greets us, his tail wagging his whole body. Kaya runs her hand over his gray ears. "*Tawts may-we*, Long Legs," she greets him. "Good morning, my dog." She scratches his ears. Kaya clearly loves dogs.

The younger woman is plucking hot stones from the fire with wooden tongs and dropping them into a basket. After a second, I realize that the basket is full of water. Is she making some kind of stone soup?

"There is much to do before the festivities tonight,"
I hear her say. She stirs the water and then drops in
pieces of fish. Not stone soup—fish soup, I realize.
She's using the hot stones to heat the water!

Kaya introduces me to the older woman. I notice
how respectfully Kaya addresses her as she explains
how we met. "I fear my new friend may have been
injured in her fall, Kautsa," Kaya says. "She does not
remember where her family is, so I brought her here."

The woman stands up, wiping her forehead with
the back of her hand. Her face is a net of deep, fine
wrinkles and her braids are gray, but her back is as
straight as a young woman's. She takes my face in her
hands and examines my head. I hold very still, but
I'm not afraid. Her touch is gentle. "You must have had
quite a tumble, young stranger," Kautsa says, looking at
my scrapes. Then she turns to Kaya. "You were right to
help her, granddaughter. *Nimíipuu* always look out for
one another."

Kautsa is Kaya's grandmother, I realize. I look at
Kaya and smile. *You know your grandmother well*, I say
to her with my eyes. *She said exactly what you said she
would*. I can tell by the spark in Kaya's face that she

understands me. Even though we just met, we seem to have our own way of "throwing words."

The other woman is Kaya's mother, whom Kaya calls Eetsa. "You are welcome here with us," Eetsa says to me warmly. Her smile is friendly, but her face is also full of concern for me.

"Kaya, our visitor looks tired. Show her to your sleeping mat so that she can rest."

"*Aa-heh*, Eetsa," Kaya says. She pushes aside the flap to the tepee and leads me inside.

❖ *Turn to page 43.*

can't rest for long. "Can I get up now?" I ask
Kaya, who has been sitting next to me quietly.

"The herbs are dry," she says, checking my arms
and forehead. "How do you feel?"

"Better," I say honestly. I don't know if it's the rest
or the medicine, but I do feel a renewed energy. I'm
also curious about the work Kaya mentioned. Kaya
cleans the dried herbs from my scrapes and helps me
up. I help her put away the soft animal hide and the
sleeping mat.

Outside the tepee, the two boys are awake and
are playing with their miniature bows and arrows.
I see now that they are twins. "These two troublesome
boys are my brothers, Wing Feather and Sparrow,"
Kaya says, tousling their hair affectionately. They look
at me curiously, without a hint of shyness. Eetsa and
Kautsa bend over the fire, feeding it more wood.

Just then, two girls approach the tepee. One walks
behind the other, holding a pinch of her dress. Both are
carrying bundles of branches on their backs. "Kaya,
have you brought us a visitor?" the older girl asks as
she places the wood near the fire.

"These are my sisters. This is Brown Deer," Kaya

gestures toward the older one. "And this is Speaking Rain," Kaya says, touching the younger girl on the shoulder. This is the adopted sister Kaya told me about. Her eyes are cloudy, and I realize that she's blind. Kaya gently helps Speaking Rain with her bundle of branches.

Kaya tells her sisters how we met. "Falling must have been very frightening," Brown Deer says, her eyes wide. "You are so courageous, being alone and away from your family."

I blush and duck my head. "Oh, no. Kaya's the courageous one," I insist. I'm not used to anyone calling me courageous.

Speaking Rain offers me a gentle smile. "Welcome. We are glad you're safe." Gracefully, she settles herself near the entrance to the tepee and picks up a pile of some sort of dyed grasses.

I hang back, suddenly shy in the middle of this big group. I'm only used to lots of people during the holidays when my grandparents and cousins all come to our house. Would it be fun to have such a big family around all the time?

"This salmon needs to be made into pemmican,"

Kautsa says to Kaya, gesturing to a mat covered with dried fish. Her voice is firm but not harsh.

"Yes, Kautsa." Kaya ducks into the tepee and comes out a moment later with a large basket that has a stone bottom. She kneels near me and uses a tool to begin mashing the salmon. I realize that it's a mortar and pestle. My mom has a smaller one that she uses to grind herbs in our kitchen at home.

A large piece of fish flies out from under Kaya's pestle as she pounds away. Kautsa puts her hand on Kaya's shoulder. "You're working too quickly, granddaughter. Go slowly and you won't waste anything."

I feel bad that Kaya's been scolded. But she doesn't seem embarrassed by her grandmother's correction. Instead, she nods and pounds more slowly. "*Katsee-yow-yow*, Kautsa." She smiles up at her grandmother, and Kautsa rubs Kaya's shoulder.

"May I help?" I ask.

Kautsa nods. She brings another stone-bottom basket from the tepee so that I can mash fish with Kaya.

I kneel next to Kaya, who adds several pieces of fish to my basket. I've used a pestle before, so I know how

to hold the club-shaped tool. Kaya and I grind the fish into a sort of mush. Then Kautsa adds a thick liquid to our bowls. I must look confused, because Kaya explains. "Oil from the salmon," she says. I watch her mix the fish and oil with her hands, and then I do the same.

"Will you eat this tonight at the festivities?" I ask.

Kaya shakes her head. "Pemmican keeps well, so it is a good food to eat when we travel. We will store it for later this summer and into the winter."

Kautsa stops to check our progress. "You are good workers," she tells us. "This will help feed the people in the seasons to come."

Kaya and I look at each other and smile from her grandmother's praise.

❖ *Turn to page 50.*

he interior of the tepee is dim and still after the bright sun and wind outside. When my eyes adjust, I see colorful bundles and beautifully woven baskets stacked neatly against the walls of the tepee and hanging from the poles that support the sides. Rolled-up mats, like the ones I saw outside, lean against the walls, which are made of more straw mats. In the middle of the clean dirt floor, a ring of stones encloses the ashes of a fire. Breezes flutter the mats that form the walls and let in little chinks of light. It's like a tent—it *is* a tent.

"You can share a sleeping mat with my sister Speaking Rain and me," Kaya says. "There's plenty of room."

"How many of you sleep here?" I ask.

Kaya lists her family members: two sisters, two brothers, her parents, *and* her grandparents.

Nine people! I try not to look shocked, but that's a lot to fit into a space that's smaller than my own bedroom!

Kaya sighs happily. "It's so cozy when everyone is together. Soon my sister Brown Deer will be old enough to marry. It will be strange to wake up and not

see her on the other side of the fire."

Kaya spreads out a large mat. Then she smooths a furry hide over the top and lays a stuffed buckskin bag on it. It takes me a minute to realize that it's a pillow.

"Kaya, you don't need to go to any trouble," I tell her. She's already done so much. But she shakes her head.

"Kautsa was right—you need rest. Here, lie down." Kaya helps me onto the soft hide. This definitely isn't like my canopy bed at home, but it's surprisingly comfortable. If this is what sleeping in a tent is like at camp, it might not be so bad.

Kaya sits beside me, and I close my eyes for a moment. I can hear the falls in the distance, and the sound is soothing from this far away. It's already cozy in the tepee, so I can't imagine another seven people crowded in here. I don't share my room at home with anyone. When I'm in it, I almost always have the door shut so that I have privacy when I'm talking to Lily on the phone or working on my crafts. I bet Kaya doesn't even know what privacy means. Is there a word for that in her language?

Voices from outside float in on the breeze. "Perhaps

she was separated from her family on the way to Celilo," I hear Eetsa saying. "They may be camped across the river and the girl has not found them yet."

"*Aa-heh*," Kautsa replies, and then hesitates. "But I do not remember seeing this girl before." There's a pause before she says, "Whatever has happened, Kaya is looking after her new friend. She is thinking of the needs of others."

I open my eyes and look at Kaya. Her cheeks turn pink from the compliment. I push myself up on my elbows. "Your grandmother is proud of you," I say.

Kaya smiles at her lap. "Kautsa tells us when we have done well . . . and when we have not, just as the other elders do," she says quietly. Then her face changes to concern. "I wish we knew where your family was. It is not good to be all alone."

"Oh, I'm used to it," I say. "I spend a lot of time by myself." That's my usual response when people ask me if I mind being an only child, but Kaya's look of concern deepens. I remind myself that Kaya's people probably don't spend much time alone. "I'm feeling better," I say, quickly changing the subject. It's true. Resting has gotten rid of any traces of dizziness. "You

helped me so quickly when I fell that I wasn't hurt as badly as I could have been."

The worry on Kaya's face lifts, and she exhales. "I'm glad! And I will be with you until we find your family—you can be my adopted sister, like Speaking Rain. Now lie back down," Kaya says gently.

I ease back onto the sleeping mat feeling as if I have a best friend in this world, too.

I'm about to ask Kaya about her sister Speaking Rain when Kautsa lifts the tepee flap and kneels next to me. "You look more rested," she says to me. "But it would be wise to ask Bear Blanket for help. She has powerful medicine."

What kind of medicine? I wonder. I'm about to insist that I'm fine, but Kautsa's firm expression and Kaya's obediently downcast eyes keep me quiet. Kaya has been quick to obey Kautsa, so I have the feeling it would be disrespectful to argue.

※ *Turn to page 48.*

I land sprawled on my carpeted bedroom floor, dressed once again in the pajamas I put on after working in my garden. I sit up and shake my head. Downstairs, Dad is still practicing scales, and Mom's phone is ringing. I'm home again, and I'm safe.

I made it back from Kaya's world, but I wish I could rewind time and go back to the moment we first saw the bear. I'd listen to Kaya this time. She knew what she was doing, and I should have trusted her. She was right there to help me, and I didn't let her.

Then I remember Kaya's final words: *Mistakes teach us to do better next time.* I think of my garden group. I made some mistakes on our first day. But I have another chance tomorrow to help the others and take care of them—just as Kaya helped and took care of me. And Ms. Wallace is there to help, too. I just have to let her.

◈ *The End* ◈

To read this story another way and see how different choices lead to a different ending, turn to page 105.

K autsa nods at Kaya, who darts out of the tent.

I can't quell the nervous rolling in my stomach. What is medicine like in Kaya's time? Mom's always telling me never to take any medicine without asking her first. What if Bear Blanket realizes I'm not really hurt from my fall? Will I be punished? Will Kaya? My stomach gives a great flop.

Relax, I tell myself. *Breathe*. I touch the cord of my bracelet, reminding myself that I can go home whenever I want. Kaya—and her family—have been kind to me so far. I want to stay and see more of how they live. I squeeze my eyes shut and summon up some of Kaya's courage. *This is the biggest adventure of your life*, I tell myself. *Be brave and go with it!* I open my eyes. It's not time to go home . . . yet.

The tepee flap lifts again, and Kaya comes in with an old, gray-haired woman. Kautsa greets her. "Bear Blanket, this young visitor needs your medicine."

Bear Blanket turns a piercing gaze on me. She is silent for such a long time that I start to get nervous. Kautsa and Kaya are still. They don't seem to mind waiting for Bear Blanket to say something.

When Bear Blanket turns to rummage in a bundle

she's brought, Kaya leans in close. "Don't worry," Kaya whispers. "Bear Blanket always keeps her mind and body clean so that she is ready to help those who need her." Kaya's voice is full of respect.

Bear Blanket turns back to me. I grope for Kaya's hand. "Stay with me?" I whisper, squeezing her hand.

"I will," she reassures me. "Don't be afraid."

Bear Blanket leans over me and lightly touches the scrapes on my forehead and arms. She mutters to herself and then dampens a small bunch of leaves with water. She presses a few leaves to each of the scrapes. The touch of her fingers is gentle and strong at the same time. "You must hold still until these dry. The sage will help heal your wounds."

I exhale as she sits back on her heels. Sage is an herb. I grow it in my garden at home. Kaya was right. There wasn't anything to worry about after all.

Suddenly, Bear Blanket's eyes narrow. "There is something else," she says.

A chill runs through me. What does Bear Blanket mean?

❖ *Turn to page 21.*

After Kaya and I spread the salmon mixture on mats to dry in the sun and wind, we wipe our oily hands on bunches of grass. Then we go over and sit with Speaking Rain.

"New Friend and I will help you with the sorting," Kaya says.

As I make piles of the dried grasses, I'm intrigued by the different shades of dark and light brown, soft green, and red. What will Speaking Rain do with them?

Happy shouts of children playing drift over to us on the breeze, mixed with the excited barking of dogs. Speaking Rain turns her head toward the sounds. "What do I hear?"

"Some of the girls are gathering to play shinny," Kaya says with excitement. "They're all on the flat-lands, with some of the dogs. Rabbit has the ball, and they've all brought their sticks."

It's some kind of a sport, I figure. The girls are dividing themselves into teams, I can see, and holding long sticks that look like the ones we use in gym to play field hockey.

"It is good to be at Celilo again," Speaking Rain

says. "It's such fun to be with all of our cousins."

"You mean all these girls are your cousins?" I ask, incredulous. I sweep my hand toward the big group playing shinny.

A look of confusion crosses Kaya's face. "Surely you remember that we are all family. We have different parents and grandparents, some of us, but that doesn't matter."

Speaking Rain nods vigorously. "We are all *Nimíipuu*, so we are one family. It has always been that way, since The People were created."

Before I can ask any more questions, a tall man strides into the camp. Kaya introduces me to her father, whom she calls Toe-ta.

"Eetsa told me of our visitor," he says in a deep voice. He looks down at me with brown eyes like Kaya's. "You are welcome here. I see that Kaya is caring for you."

He turns to Kaya. "Little daughter, we have just brought in a new group of horses. They're being held north of the flatlands, and they need some training. You are a strong rider. Would you like to help?"

I can tell that Kaya is pleased that her father has

asked her to help. But she turns to me. "What would you like to do?" she asks.

I glance at the grasses we've been sorting. I'd love to learn what Speaking Rain is going to do with them. I also think that Kaya may want to play shinny, which sounds like fun. We could do that if we stay in camp. But I've never been on a horse before, and I don't have the faintest idea how to train one. This is my chance to try it.

> ❖ *To stay in camp,*
> *turn to page 58.*

> ❖ *To go train horses,*
> *turn to page 55.*

B ack at camp, Kaya and I take Toe-ta's stallion and the chestnut horse to the pasture on the flatland. We walk slowly together, the lead-ropes drooping in our fingers. I feel an unaccustomed ache in my arms and shoulders. It doesn't feel bad, though— it feels like a reminder of everything I've done on this amazing day.

Kaya and I slip the halters off the horses and watch them join the rest of the herd. The summer sun is setting in a fluffy bed of gold- and rose-colored clouds. The distant roar of the falls mingles with the peaceful evening sounds of the herd. If I concentrate, I can hear the little clicks and crunches as the horses bite off mouthfuls of grass. I have my friend beside me and the warm memory of the help she and Toe-ta gave me. I feel filled up, as if I can't hold a single drop more of contentment. It's been a wonderful day, but I'm ready to go home.

"Kaya, I remember where I need to go to find my family," I say.

She sighs and nods. "I knew you would remember soon. I'm glad your memories have returned, but I will miss you."

"I'll miss you too." My voice catches a little. "But now we each have new memories—of our time together today. *Katsee-yow-yow.*" I hold out my hand and she takes it. The sun sends long golden rays around her head.

Kaya's long eyelashes are wet with unshed tears. "*Katsee-yow-yow* to you, my patient friend. You've taught me that lesson well."

My throat swells so that I can't speak. Instead, I squeeze Kaya's hands, then turn and walk slowly toward the river. I turn to wave. Kaya is silhouetted at the top of the rise, her braids and dress blowing in the evening wind, the ruby-and-violet-streaked sky behind her. *Thank you, Kaya, for showing me how beautiful our country is. Thank you for showing me that I don't have to be afraid of the outdoors and that I can ask for help—and offer help, too.* I'm eager to share Kaya's wisdom with my garden group. And now I can't wait to go to camp with Lily.

❖ *The End* ❖

To read this story another way and see how different choices lead to a different ending, turn back to page 96.

I've always been fascinated by horses, even though I'm a little bit afraid of them, too. But then I hear Lily's voice in my head. *You need some more adventure!* This is my chance. I take a deep breath. "I'd like to help with the training," I say.

"*Tawts!*" Kaya smiles with excitement. "We're ready, Toe-ta."

Kaya and I follow Toe-ta out of the camp and up the steep bluffs until the land flattens out. A large horse herd grazes out there in the brisk wind that blows up from the gorge. "We're training *all* these horses?" I ask Kaya, keeping my voice low. I don't want Toe-ta to hear me, in case I say something that makes it obvious I'm not *Nimíipuu*.

Kaya looks at me with concern, but her tone is kind. "These are our horses. We'll catch our mounts here to ride out to the new herd. These horses are very well trained already. They're the best and fastest horses at Celilo—and the most beautiful."

Toe-ta turns around from the horse he's bridling. "I've told you before not to boast, Kaya." He fixes her with a stern gaze. "We respect all animals—and our friends who have trained them."

Kaya drops her eyes and bites her lip. "I am sorry, Toe-ta." She pats the shoulder of the horse next to her, not looking at anyone.

When Toe-ta turns back to his horse, I put my hand on Kaya's back. "Once, I was showing a friend a new bracelet-weaving design. I told her that even though it was really complicated, I could do it better than anyone. My mother heard me and got upset with me, just like Toe-ta did with you now," I say, hoping to make Kaya feel better.

Kaya is listening carefully. "What did she say?"

"She told me that bragging is selfish, like grabbing more than your share at a meal."

Kaya nods. "I get a sick feeling in my stomach when I've done something wrong."

"Me too!" I look at Kaya and feel our bond tighten.

Kaya quickly slips a twisted rope into the mouth of a small chestnut-colored horse and climbs up onto a small log nearby. "You can ride double with me," she says. She throws her leg over the back of the horse and hoists herself up.

There's no saddle. We're going to ride bareback. I don't know much about horseback riding, but I'm

pretty sure bareback is more difficult.

"Are you ready?" Kaya asks.

I stare up at the chestnut, who doesn't seem so small all of a sudden. How will I get on the horse? I swallow hard and put my hand up to the scrape on my forehead. I think of Kaya fearlessly flinging herself onto the edge of the riverbank to grab a falling stranger. If she can do that, I should be able to do this.

Kaya is watching me with concern. "You've had a hard time today, New Friend. Do you need help?"

I nod with relief.

"Toe-ta!" Kaya calls. "New Friend needs help."

Toe-ta comes over. "Climb up on the log," he says, and when I do, he tells me to raise one knee.

Is this some kind of gymnastics act? I expected him to just lift me onto the horse. Instead, he takes my raised knee in his two hands and lifts. Feeling myself boosted up, I instinctively grab Kaya's waist and scramble up onto the warm, slippery, moving mass of horse. I'm up!

❧ *Turn to page 62.*

'd like to stay in camp," I say quietly, hoping I haven't disappointed my new friend.

Kaya breaks into a wide smile. "*Tawts*," she says. "We can keep working with Speaking Rain."

Toe-ta nods, and he and Eetsa walk out of camp together. Brown Deer takes Wing Feather and Sparrow with her to the stream to get water, while Kautsa settles herself off to one side of the tepee. She pulls long strands of what looks like hemp from a basket and begins braiding it into rope, her fingers moving quickly.

Kaya and I turn back to the grasses. Speaking Rain is weaving them together to make a flat, flexible bag.

"Speaking Rain's weaving is fine and tight," Kaya says with admiration.

As I watch, the grass strands seem to leap and twist themselves into place under Speaking Rain's nimble fingers. "It's beautiful," I say, admiring the pattern, a small zigzag of dark brown fibers against a pale brown background.

Speaking Rain stops for a moment and runs her fingertips over the finished section. "*Katsee-yow-yow.*"

"Do you think you could show me how to do that pattern?"

"*Aa-heh*," Speaking Rain says. "This is the design from Rattlesnake's back." Slowly and patiently, Speaking Rain describes what she's doing as she weaves. I watch, amazed that she can do this work by touch alone.

Kaya picks up another half-finished bag, also flat and woven of dried grass. She gives a small sigh. "I'm not good at weaving. I get impatient or I daydream, and then I have holes and lumps." A little shadow seems to pass over her round, cheerful face as she touches the grassy strands sticking out of the end of the bag.

Speaking Rain reaches out to Kaya. "Your weaving will get better."

Kautsa looks up from her work. "Mistakes are not bad, Kaya. They teach us to do better next time."

Kaya's face lightens at her grandmother's words. "I don't know if I'll ever be able to weave patterns as well as Speaking Rain. But if I work as hard as she does, I will improve."

I'm impressed by how Kaya and her sister pay such close attention to each other and care about what the other is doing. I can't help thinking of Rachel and Sarah and Greta back at home. The members of our garden

group don't seem to care what anyone else is doing. We don't encourage one another the way Kaya's family does, I think, looking around at the peaceful, busy scene.

Suddenly, I realize that Kaya is watching me. She touches my neck. "You don't have a necklace." She wears a beautiful one of blue, red, and green porcupine quills. White beads space out the quills. "Do you want to make one? You can wear it to the festivities tonight."

It would be wonderful to wear a special necklace. "Yes, I'd love to make one," I say.

Kaya goes to the tepee and returns with some very fine cord, just like the kind I use at home. "Here are some bone beads you can string." She holds out three long white beads. They look as though they're carved from smooth bone.

I begin weaving the cord together, just the way I was doing before I came here. Kaya leans over and watches me as I make a series of tiny knots in the cord to hold the beads of my new necklace. It will make a cool bumpy pattern around them when I'm done.

"I've never seen that pattern before," she says. "Little knots are all around the beads, holding them in place like a pod holding a seed," she says, guiding

Speaking Rain's fingers to the necklace so that she can feel the pattern.

"You must have practiced many times to master such a pattern," Speaking Rain says to me. "I can tell you are patient by how quietly you sit while you work."

Kautsa smiles over at me. "I've noticed the same about our visitor. She must know that a quiet body and a quiet mind can make beautiful objects."

I blush, overcome with the unexpected praise, and finger the necklace in my lap.

◈ *Turn to page 65.*

I hold tightly to Kaya's waist with both arms. Following Toe-ta, who has mounted a big stallion, we set off through the rolling, grassy hills away from the river valley. My eyes are shut tightly against the wind. The horse's muscles bunch and release beneath me as he canters on and on. I grip tightly with my legs, trying not to slip off.

After a few minutes, the sound of the falls lessens and I can hear the rhythmic, steady thud of the hooves. The wind dies down, and I can open my eyes. I'm riding a horse for the first time! Kaya makes me feel safe, and a thrill runs all through me.

"I love riding out here," Kaya says. I can feel the words vibrating through her back. "The color of the grasses changes with the wind—and the sky is so wide. *Hun-ya-wat* the Creator made such a beautiful land for all creatures to live in." In her voice, I can hear how much she loves her homeland.

Kaya's words are like an invisible thread binding us a little closer together. I feel the same way when I'm in my garden. I like watching how plants change and grow and change again. "I know just what you mean," I tell Kaya as we ride together.

I take a deep breath, relaxing even further, and really look around for the first time. I'm amazed at how much farther I can see from up here. The soft browns and yellows of the grasses and earth are studded with clumps of soft green sagebrush. If I twist around, I can just see the soft silver mist above the falls we've left behind. "It's beautiful!" I exclaim.

"*Aa-heh*," Kaya agrees. "This is my happiest place—here on a horse's back." She reaches down and pats the chestnut's neck.

"Look!" I say. In the sky ahead of us, a bald eagle folds its wings and plummets to the earth like a black stone dropped from the heavens. "It'll smash itself!" I gasp.

Kaya just laughs. "No, it won't!" The eagle is already rising from the earth with something—some small animal—caught in its talons. "Eagles are strong and courageous," Kaya says over her shoulder. "This is a sign to give us strength and bravery for what lies ahead."

"*I* need some courage, but I don't think you do. After all, you saved my life," I remind her. "I can't imagine you being afraid."

"I am, sometimes," Kaya says quickly. "There are dangers to be aware of—wild animals and fires and enemy raids. But I am more afraid of not doing my work well. I want to be ready to meet the challenges I'm given. I try to be strong so that I might be a leader of our people one day," she says thoughtfully.

"I am not a good leader," I confess. "I would rather do things on my own."

"Bear Blanket often goes off by herself," Kaya says. "Being alone makes her stronger for our people. But she always comes back and helps others. Being alone can be good—what matters is that you come back."

"You are good at helping others, Kaya," I say.

After a pause, Kaya quietly replies, "I try to be."

As we ride in silence, I think of Rachel and Greta and Sarah. How could I be better at helping them?

❖ *Turn to page 67.*

etsa comes back to the camp. "Kaya, will you and New Friend gather some of the salmon eggs from the drying spot on the hillside?"

"*Aa-heh*, we will do that," Kaya says quickly. She doesn't even seem to mind putting down her work. I think about all the times I've grumbled at my mom when she asks me to stop crafting to set the table or help her make dinner.

Kaya takes the basket and leads me out of camp. We walk quickly, and in about five minutes we're climbing the hillside that rises from the riverbank. At the top, there's a patchwork of straw mats covered with tiny pink balls. Those are the salmon eggs, which look like the caviar Dad has once in a while. It's a very special treat because a small amount is really expensive. I wonder what he'd think if he could see all these salmon eggs just sitting here on the top of a hill. Does Kaya have any idea how much all this would cost in a grocery store? Does she even know what money is?

Kaya plumps down on her knees and begins running her hand over the eggs. "We only gather the ones that are dry," she says to me. She scoops a few into the basket.

Tentatively, I kneel beside her and help pick the eggs that are ready. As we work, I realize how far out of my usual routine I am. I'm out in the middle of nature, wearing a buckskin dress, picking dried fish eggs while the river roars below us. Normally I'd be nervous in such an unfamiliar situation. But I'm really enjoying myself and this time with Kaya.

"Kautsa gives me salmon eggs to trade sometimes," Kaya says, carefully moving the damp eggs to the side and spreading them out again. "I may be able to get an unusual bead or a pretty shell from the people who come from the place where the big river flows into the sea."

"So the eggs are worth a lot?" I ask.

Kaya nods vigorously. "Oh, yes," she says, placing more dried eggs in the basket. "For a good trade, you have to offer something of equal value in return."

Kaya's people may not have money or stores, but it sounds as if trading is as common as shopping. What would I trade if there was something I really wanted in Kaya's world?

❧ *Turn to page 69.*

We ride for a little while longer and then stop at a wide, grassy spot. I see a small herd of horses clustered together with a few riders circling them. Toe-ta dismounts and quickly ties his stallion a short distance away. Kaya and I slide off the chestnut. My legs are trembling from the exertion of staying on the horse.

"There's Jumps Back, one of my uncles." Kaya points to one of the riders. "And that's Raven and Squirrel." She nods toward two boys who look to be about our age. One of them breaks away from the group and trots in a fast circle around us.

"Can't your friend ride her own horse?" he asks in a pesky tone, his dark eyes snapping.

I quake a little inside. Can he tell that I'm not really *Nimíipuu*? Before Kaya or I can say anything, he grins at us merrily and wheels around, trotting to the herd.

"Squirrel likes to tease," Kaya warns.

Toe-ta comes up to us. "The horses need to get used to people. They will need to learn to carry riders and to be led. Choose what you want to work on first. If you need me," Toe-ta adds, "I'm here to help."

Kaya turns to me. "Do you want to ride or stay on the ground?"

Before I can say anything, Squirrel breaks in again. "This stranger's afraid to ride alone!" he says, grinning. "She'd better work with an old horse. There are some slow ones back at camp!"

I shrink back, wishing I could think of something to say to Squirrel, but I can't—just as I couldn't with Sarah and Rachel in the garden.

"Don't be unkind," Kaya scolds. "New Friend has been injured. Let her work at her own pace," she says before turning her back on Squirrel.

Kaya's good to defend me, and it's clear she's not letting Squirrel bother her. I try to do the same, but Squirrel has gotten under my skin.

◈ *To get on the horse to show that you're not afraid, turn to page 79.*

◈ *To ignore Squirrel and work on the ground, turn to page 71.*

When we've filled our basket, Kaya and I head back to camp. As we make our way carefully down the slope, I realize that I can see all the way to the edge of the horizon, where the sky touches the earth. It's breathtaking. The sky is the deepest, most pure blue I've ever seen, and the gold, green, and dusky-purple grasses rustle in the strong wind. I pick up a round pink stone and put it in the pouch that hangs around my waist. It reminds me of the color of the shell in my bracelet. It will look pretty once it's been polished.

When we get to the river, I study the men and boys who are fishing. Many stand on rocky outcroppings along the shore. They hold long, thin poles that they stab into the water. I watch one man pull his pole from the water with a big, wiggly salmon attached to the end. He must have *speared* the fish!

Other men are standing on wooden platforms built out over the falls. They're wielding big nets with long handles, and they seem to hover above the churning water as they lean into the white spray of foam.

"Kaya, isn't that dangerous?" I ask as I watch a man dip his net down into the powerful water and then pull it up with a giant, thrashing fish caught in the fibers.

"Aa-heh," Kaya says with a respectful tone. "Our men must be very strong to fish against the force of the current and lift the heavy salmon."

I'm about to ask Kaya how the fishermen keep their balance when I see a man suddenly lose his net and pinwheel his arms. He topples off the edge of the platform and disappears toward the rushing water.

"Kaya!" I scream, pointing to the empty platform. "Someone just fell!"

❖ *Turn to page 32.*

turn my back on Squirrel and try to ignore him. "Let's work on leading for a while," I tell Kaya. That'll give me a chance to steady my wobbly legs.

"*Tawts*," Kaya agrees. "Now, which horse should we work with?" We walk around the edge of the herd. Brown horses, black horses, horses with white faces and gray spots, horses with brown faces and white spots—I'm dizzy with all the colors, tossing manes, tails flicking flies, backs and rumps shining in the sunlight.

I glance at Kaya, wondering if she can sense the nervousness fluttering in my belly. There are so many horses, and they're all so big and wild. I can't tell Kaya how I feel, though. Kaya thinks I'm *Nimíipuu* and if there's anything I've learned about *Nimíipuu* today, it's that they're very comfortable around—and on—horses!

A young black-and-white horse stands near the edge of the group, with its head up. Its shiny coat and spotted rump gleam in the sun, and the wind twists its silky mane up off its fine, graceful neck. As we walk by, the horse spots us and lets out a nicker, a friendly little sound. It has a perfect white star on its forehead. It paws the ground and then nickers again. Kaya stops.

She and the horse gaze at each other. Then, as if calling out, the horse lifts its nose and lets out a long, ringing whinny. Kaya puts her fingers in her mouth and answers with a low whistle. The young horse breaks from the herd and canters up to Kaya, stopping in front of her. It lowers its head and pushes it against Kaya's leg.

Kaya and I look at each other in astonishment and delight. "Hello, Little Girl," Kaya greets her. The filly responds by nudging Kaya's shoulder. Kaya gently places a hand on her neck. "I'm glad to meet you, too. I'm Kaya." The filly bobs her head and snorts softly.

I watch them together, enchanted. If I didn't know better, I could swear the filly was talking back to Kaya.

Kaya gently loops a rope halter around the filly's nose and behind her ears. The little horse tosses her head at the unfamiliar feel, and Kaya immediately loosens the rope a bit. "There, there," she croons. "Don't be afraid. I'll take care of you." The horse must sense Kaya's tenderness, because she relaxes and lowers her head.

I can't help being impressed. "Kaya, it's as if you two can speak to each other!" I say.

"*Aa-heh!* Kautsa says every creature has wisdom to

share with us. So I try to listen very carefully—to the horses and the dogs that live with us."

I haven't been around animals as much as Kaya has, but I think I understand what she means. When I'm working in my garden, I seem to know what my plants need, almost as if they can talk to me. That's why I talk to them, too.

◈ *Turn to page 83.*

When Kaya and I return to camp, Eetsa is working quickly to pack several bundles. "Falling Leaf is about to have her baby," she says. "I must go to help. Kautsa has gone to the stream, but she will return soon. Kaya, it is your job to look after your brothers."

Kaya puts the basket of fish eggs down. "Here, boys," she says without hesitating. "Come sit with us, and we'll make some horses for you." Sparrow and Wing Feather, their eyes bright, crouch next to her.

Kaya reaches into a small basket and pulls out a handful of what looks like straw. Her fingers move quickly, and in a few minutes, she hands Wing Feather a little horse made out of the straw.

"Me too! I want one too!" Sparrow says, hopping up and down.

"I'll make you one," I offer shyly. "Kaya, will you help me?"

Kaya nods, and the boys watch my hands work while Kaya tells me step-by-step how to twist and bend the straw. The boys have so much fun watching that Wing Feather asks me to make him a second horse.

"Me too," Sparrow cries. By the time I've made my third horse, I'm pretty good at it!

The boys take their horses to the edge of camp to play. With the boys entertained, I'm tempted to go back to the weaving project I started before Kaya and I went to gather salmon eggs. Just as I'm about to suggest it, Brown Deer spreads out an animal hide and stakes it to the ground. Next to her are some shells filled with what look like different colors of paint and some long sticks. It's some kind of art project. I wonder if she would let me help her.

Suddenly, I realize that the twins are no longer at the edge of the camp—or anywhere in the clearing. "Kaya?" I ask, feeling a wave of panic. "Where are the boys?"

◈ *Turn to page 85.*

ould you mind if we painted for a while? " I ask Kaya.

"I would like that," Kaya says.

The three of us kneel around the hide. "I've already painted it with a fish-egg mixture," Brown Deer tells us. "That will make it waterproof so that it will be good for storage."

"Perhaps you will trade this parfleche with some-one here at Celilo," Speaking Rain says from her spot in the shade.

Parfleche, I repeat to myself as I trace the smooth, damp surface with my fingertips. I wonder what it will look like when we're done. Were those colorful pouches in Kaya's tepee a type of parfleche?

Kaya lays several long, slim sticks in a pattern on the hide. She touches a bone tool to the paint in one of the shells and begins tracing lines, using the sticks as a guide.

When she's finished tracing a pattern, Kaya turns to me. "Will you choose the color for this section?" she asks, handing me a small tool that looks like a piece of bone.

"Yes!" I say eagerly. I dip the tool in the shell filled

with green paint and watch in fascination as the porous bone soaks up the paint. It spreads perfectly when I stroke it on the hide. A paintbrush without any bristles!

Wing Feather and Sparrow pop out from the tepee and run over to us. Sparrow almost steps in the paint in his haste. "Can we help?" Wing Feather screeches to a halt when he sees what we are doing.

Kaya takes their hands and pulls them down next to her, one on each side. "That wasn't a very long rest," she says playfully.

"I want to paint!" Sparrow picks up one of the painting tools.

Kaya gently takes it from his hand and lays it down. "Tell our new friend the meaning of the colors instead. Remember? What does red mean?"

"Red is for the sunrise," Wing Feather pipes up, his little face shining. Both boys are sitting alertly now, their eyes fixed on Kaya.

"White is the snow and winter," Sparrow says. "Isn't it, sister?"

"*Aa-heh*, that's right. And blue is the sky, where *Hun-ya-wat* lives," Kaya says.

"Brown is for the earth," Speaking Rain puts in.

"And green is for all the things that grow." She smiles. "I used to love it when Eetsa would let us help her paint and she would tell us all the colors."

I lay the tool down. "There." The triangular section is nicely filled in. I admire the glowing sea green. "Where did you get this paint?"

"River algae," Kaya tells me. "Do you remember that? It makes the best green."

Before I can answer, I hear a baby cry out, from somewhere close by, a high, trembling wail. It's not an ordinary cry—even I can tell that. Speaking Rain hears it too and raises her head.

"Something's wrong," she says.

I nod. "I'll go see what it is."

I jump to my feet and run off between the tepees in the direction of the cry. As soon as I see what it is, I call for Kaya. "I need your help!"

❖ *Turn to page 98.*

et's work on some riding," I tell Kaya, making sure Squirrel can hear me.

She smiles. "*Tawts!* This little one looks as if she wants to get to know us." She loops a light rope halter over a young black horse with a white star shape on her forehead and a spotted white rump. We spend a few minutes patting her soft muzzle and stroking her ears. I see Kaya scratch her right under her jaw, so I scratch hard at the rough hair there. The horse stretches her neck out and half-closes her eyes with pleasure. I've seen cats do this before. I had no idea a horse would, too!

"She's so sweet, Kaya," I say, giving the horse a final scratch and a firm pat on the neck. I never thought that I'd be patting a horse like this—and that the horse would like it. I don't even feel scared.

"She wants to work with us, I can tell." Kaya gazes into the horse's face. "She knows we're her friends." There's something familiar about the focused intensity in her face as she gazes at the horse. She feels the same connection to these animals that I do to my plants, I realize suddenly. I always feel at home with my hands in the dirt—it seems as if Kaya feels the same with her hands on a horse.

Kaya places a rope bit in the filly's mouth. "We'll teach her mounting first," Kaya says. "Our horses have to stand quietly until the rider gives the signal. Would you like to mount first?"

"Oh, no, no, you go first." I back away a few steps and watch Kaya closely.

She runs forward a few steps, then grasps the horse's mane with both hands, and in the same motion throws her leg up and bellies over her. The first few times, the filly snorts and dances a bit, but Kaya soothes her with pats and tries again.

After about half a dozen mounts, she turns to me. "Why don't you try? It's good for her to get used to different riders."

I step forward, hearing my heart thudding in my ears. How did that little horse get so big all of a sudden? I'm nervous. Kaya can't know I've never done this before.

I take a running step, then stop. Toe-ta has joined us. "Let me help you." He steps by the horse's head. "A new horse will feel more secure if someone holds her head while another person mounts." I can see the filly relax as soon as he puts his hand on her nose.

Kaya nods. "*Aa-heh*, Toe-ta." He steps away and Kaya takes a gentle hold of the rope halter that the horse wears.

Then Toe-ta signals me. "Go ahead."

I run forward as Kaya did, but without much conviction. Instead of jumping onto the horse's back, I collide with its side and slither embarrassingly to the ground in a heap. I hear a snicker as I pick myself up and look over to see Squirrel standing nearby, his hands on his hips, clearly enjoying my clumsiness. My face flames, and I wish I could crawl right under that horse and stay there.

"Squirrel," Toe-ta says. "The herd is wandering. Gather it together."

Squirrel turns to go, but throws one last gleeful grin over his shoulder. I scowl at him.

"Now, run with confidence. Remember that you and the horse are partners," Toe-ta tells me. "*Nimíipuu* are one with their horses. We love and care for them and they love and care for us. Let this be the start of that friendship."

Toe-ta's words make me smile. That's exactly what I've seen in Kaya today!

"You can do it!" Kaya calls.

I run forward, powerfully this time, and leap just before I reach the filly. This time I reach her mane and almost scramble up before I fall to the ground again. The horse snorts and dances to one side.

"There now," Kaya strokes her nose and murmurs soothingly. "This is new for you. You are learning quickly, though." The horse bobs her head and leans against Kaya's arm.

"She likes you, Kaya," I say. "I can tell that she trusts you already."

She smiles at my praise. "*Katsee-yow-yow*. We won't be able to learn at all if we don't trust one another— you, and me, and the horse."

"We need to respect the horses as well," Toe-ta says. "And they will respect us." He turns toward the other side of the clearing. "Keep trying, New Friend. Don't give up."

❖ *Turn to page 88.*

K aya and I work with Little Girl for a long time. We ask her to walk beside us calmly and to stop when we stop. We agree that the horse is very smart.

Kaya has just removed Little Girl's halter when I hear hoofbeats in the distance, like drums. Whoever is approaching is galloping fast. Toe-ta shouts from the other side of the herd. Suddenly, everything is chaos and confusion. A group of riders tears toward us, bent low over their horses, their braids flying. They don't look friendly.

Jumps Back yells, "Raiders! Enemies!"

"Run, hide!" Toe-ta shouts as he gallops past us on his swift stallion.

"Kaya!" I cry out. Fear sweeps over me, and I grab for my friend's strong hand.

"This way!" Kaya pulls me away from the horses through the clouds of dust. Arrows zing past us. The raiders are shooting at the men—and at us!

The raiders shout to one another in a language I can't understand. They surround us, spread out in a circle around the herd, and close in rapidly. There is dust everywhere as confused horses paw the dirt, neighing in a panic. I can't think over the voices of Toe-ta and the other men, who are trying to fight off the invaders.

Kaya and I are trying to make our way to the cover of a large rock when Kaya stops suddenly.

"What are you doing?" I scream over the noise and commotion. "Toe-ta said to hide!"

Kaya's looking at the frightened horses. "Little Girl! We've got to help her!" she cries.

❖ *To pull Kaya behind the rock,*
   turn to page 90.

❖ *To try to save the horse,*
   turn to page 97.

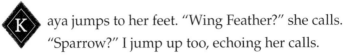aya jumps to her feet. "Wing Feather?" she calls. "Sparrow?" I jump up too, echoing her calls.

"Would they run off?" I ask anxiously. We're not near the river, but I think of the small boys tumbling into the water.

Kaya shakes her head. "They like to play tricks," she says. "They may be hiding."

Kaya and Brown Deer and I search the camp while Speaking Rain calls to the boys. Just when I think that something truly bad has happened, I spy two sets of little moccasins behind the tepee. Thank goodness! I nudge Kaya, and she nods. We creep around the side of the tepee, catching the twins on their hands and knees with their backs to us, looking around the other side.

"Found you!" We pounce on them, and they both shriek with delight. Kaya scoops up Sparrow and carries him to the front of the tepee again, while Wing Feather follows.

Relieved, Brown Deer and Speaking Rain go back to their tasks. I'm hoping Kaya and I can join them, but Sparrow has other ideas.

"We want to play a game," Sparrow demands. Kaya frowns as if she's not sure what to do.

"I have an idea," I say. "Do you have a ball?"

Sparrow nods, and he and Wing Feather scurry to get one.

I call Long Legs over from his resting spot in the shade. "Let's see if we can toss this ball to one another without Long Legs getting it." My next-door neighbors have a dog, and I've seen them do this with a Frisbee.

The boys love it, and Long Legs is a great player. He's eager but gentle with the boys. We play until Long Legs is panting and the boys are tired from running.

A tall girl about our age comes into camp. "Hello, Kaya!" she calls. "There is news that you have a new friend. Would you two like to play shinny?" she asks.

"*Aa-heh*, Rabbit!" Kaya says. "But we are caring for my brothers. We will play later."

After Rabbit leaves, the boys demand a new game. Kaya and I look at each other. We seem to be out of ideas. That's when Kautsa comes back from the stream.

"Boys, come inside the tepee with me and rest for a moment. I will tell you a story while I work," says Kautsa.

The twins scramble inside, and Kaya looks at her grandmother gratefully. "Now we can rest for a

moment, too," Kaya says to me.

"Would you like to help me paint this buffalo hide?" Brown Deer asks. "Or are you going to play shinny?"

Kaya looks at me. "It's your choice," she says.

I really want to paint with Brown Deer, but I know how much Kaya would like to play shinny.

◈ To paint the buffalo hide,
  turn to page 76.

◈ To play shinny,
  turn to page 91.

I'm determined that we'll get this, both the horse and me. *Wheels.* Dad's nickname for me echoes in my mind as I run across the grass. This is like learning to ride the bike. Except not a bike.

"You're a hard worker!" Kaya says admiringly when we stop for a rest. My face, legs, and arms are caked with dust, and I'm panting. Kaya's world is full of hard physical work. Kaya seems used to it, but I'm hot and tired! I'd love a cool shower in an air-conditioned bathroom. A little pang goes through me at the thought of home.

"Well, I really want to train this horse," I say, accepting the water bag Kaya holds out. Sweet coolness flows down my parched throat.

"You haven't given up," Kaya sighs. "Kautsa says I would be better at some of my tasks if I was more patient."

"I sometimes feel impatient," I confess. "But if I try to just focus on what I'm doing and not think about anything else, the impatience goes away."

Kaya only shakes her head. "My thoughts seem to fly around like swallows."

"This is what I do when I need to calm down and

focus." I close my eyes and take five long, slow breaths, inhaling and exhaling evenly. Then I open my eyes. "You breathe in, then hold it, then breathe out, then hold it, all for the same amount of time. If you concentrate on breathing, you stop thinking about what's bothering you."

Kaya tries it while the herd stamps and shifts all around her. When she opens her eyes, she smiles. "You are very wise, New Friend."

I smile back. It feels nice to be able to help Kaya— I'm glad she needs me too. And I'm glad I wasn't afraid to work with the horses. I turn around to see if Squirrel has noticed. But I can't find him.

"Kaya? Where's Squirrel?" I ask her.

She scans the landscape. "I don't see him. He couldn't have disappeared!"

We look at each other and at the same moment realize that he has.

◈ *Turn to page 95.*

I hold Kaya's wrist as tightly as I can. "Toe-ta told us to hide," I whisper urgently. "We should listen to him."

"You're right," she says. We dive behind a big rock.

The raiders have spread out to try to drive away the herd. The horses are all circling and plunging in confusion. Suddenly Little Girl runs out of the chaos. She's practically in front of us. So is one of the raiders. He's looking away, shouting to another raider, so I don't think he sees us.

"Little Girl!" Kaya cries. "We can't let them take her. I'll call to her. She'll come to my whistle."

"But the enemy could see us," I tell Kaya. "We should wait until it's safe and then go back to camp for help."

"The raiders—and Little Girl—will be long gone by then," Kaya says.

❧ To tell Kaya to whistle to the filly,
  turn to page 109.

❧ To run back to the camp,
  turn to page 103.

Let's play shinny," I say. Kaya is delighted. She and I run to a flat spot a short distance from the camp, where a bunch of other girls have gathered. When Kaya hands me a curved stick, my stomach sinks a little. Shinny sounded like fun when Kaya mentioned it earlier, but now I'm worried that I'll embarrass myself—and my friend. I'm not great at sports.

I look up to see Kaya studying my face. She seems to know what I'm thinking. "Don't worry," she says. "You've only forgotten for a little while. When we start playing, you'll remember."

Kaya thinks my near-fall is the reason I don't know what to do, I realize.

Kaya drops a ball in between us. "Let's play a bit, just the two of us, before we join the others," she suggests. She gently reminds me of the rules. There are two teams. Each team has a goal and has to get the ball through the other team's goal to win.

"Now, this is how you pass the ball." She taps the leather ball with her curved stick. "You want to pass it right to your teammate. Here, you try."

I give the ball a little tap.

"Yes! Gentle taps for passing," Kaya praises me.

"I did it right?" I've never done anything right involving a ball before.

"*Aa-heh*. Here, I'll stand back some. Now pass it to me again."

I hit the ball to her from a little farther away.

"*Tawts!*" Kaya calls. She comes back toward me. "Let's work on scoring. You need a strong smack for that one."

I look at Kaya with admiration. "You're a good leader," I tell her, thinking of my own hesitation with the garden group at home. "You're spending all this time with me, just so I can learn, when you could be off with the others, having fun playing the game."

"I am having fun with you," Kaya says happily.

Kaya sets up a little goal for me, and I practice shooting the ball past her while she tries to block me. Over and over, her stick stops my ball. I'm sweating now, and little wisps of hair are sticking to my forehead. But I've forgotten everything except my stick, the ball, and the goal.

"Let's rest!" Kaya calls. "You're working hard!"

I shake my head. "No, I want to get this," I say, not taking my eyes off the shot I'm lining up. "Just a

little longer—" I smack the ball with a satisfying *thwack,* and to my joy, the leather sphere shoots across the grass right past Kaya and into the little stick-lined goal box.

"You did it!" Kaya cries.

"I did, didn't I?" I can hardly believe it myself.

"You didn't give up," Kaya says as we sink down under a small tree. "You tried and tried until you got it. I don't always do that."

"I don't always try as hard as I should, either," I admit, thinking about the garden group.

Kaya sighs. "Kautsa often tells me that I can't do anything perfectly the first time." She braids a tuft of dry grass near her knee. "I have to practice," she says as she lets the braid unravel.

"I don't always like practicing, either," I tell Kaya. I reach over and re-braid the grass tuft, finishing it with a knot at the end so that it won't unbraid. "My mom says that if I want to get better at something, practicing is the only way to do it."

"You're remembering something about your family!" Kaya cries. "Your memory must be coming back."

"Perhaps it is," I say. Kaya's enthusiasm is so genuine that I have to smile. I get to my feet. "I'll guard the goal, and you try to shoot past me."

"Watch out for this one!" Kaya says as she whacks the ball. I try to block it, but I miss. I run after it as it bounces past me and disappears between some nearby tepees. I'm about to pounce on it when I see something that draws me up short.

"Kaya?" I call back. "I think you should come here."

◈ *Turn to page 98.*

quirrel!" Kaya calls. "Are you here?"

There is no answer. No one else is close enough to realize that he's gone. Then I see a stand of juniper trees shaking. I nudge Kaya and point.

We let the black-and-white filly go back to the herd. Then we creep over and peer through the screen of branches. Squirrel hasn't heard us calling, but he's there behind the trees with a gray horse. The gray has a rope halter on. Squirrel is yanking at the halter and saying something in an angry voice to the horse.

"She must have strayed off from the herd," Kaya murmurs to me as we crouch in the spiny bushes. "But it looks as if she won't budge." Squirrel yanks again at the gray's halter, and Kaya winces.

"We should never touch our horses disrespectfully," Kaya whispers. Squirrel pulls hard on the halter, but the gray sets her feet and raises her head high. He tugs her head back and forth, and she snorts and flattens her ears. Dark rivulets of sweat track down her shoulders to her chest.

"Move!" Squirrel slaps the horse on the shoulder with the loose end of the rope, and I press my hand over my mouth to keep from gasping. He raises his hand toward the horse's head as if to hit her.

We both gasp. "We have to get your father!" I whisper.

"No, I'll talk to Squirrel," Kaya says.

> ◈ *To tell Toe-ta about Squirrel,*
> *turn to page 100.*

> ◈ *To let Kaya talk to Squirrel,*
> *turn to page 106.*

'm about to argue with Kaya, but the look on her face tells me she won't change her mind. Instead I say, "Tell me what to do."

"Follow me," she shouts.

Kaya and I run toward a knot of horses. I do what Kaya's doing and wave my arms wildly, hoping to drive them away from the enemies.

Kaya spots Little Girl and struggles to get close enough to throw a rope over her neck. She's almost there when I spot a raider turning his horse toward Kaya.

"Kaya!" I shriek, pointing. She pauses, and I can tell she wants to reach out for Little Girl. But I can't let the raider see us. I grab Kaya, and we dive back behind the rock. We both watch as Little Girl gallops past us, nostrils flaring, her eyes wild with fear.

Another horse pounds up behind us, with Toe-ta riding low over the neck. "Girls, run, get help from camp!" Toe-ta shouts. "There are too many of them!" Then he turns to follow the raiders.

Kaya and I take off running as fast as we can.

❖ *Turn to page 103.*

Kaya comes running and sees what I see: a young woman kneeling on the ground, holding a wailing baby. "We were returning from the salmon drying racks when Little Branch started crying," the woman said, clutching the baby. "That's when I noticed she was burning with fever. Please help me!"

Kaya and I look at each other over the woman's head. I can feel the fear and distress coming from the mother in waves. "Don't be troubled, Rushing Brook," Kaya says. "Come into our tepee, and I will fetch Bear Blanket." Her voice is steady and soothing, and I can see the woman relax.

We rush past Kaya's brothers and sisters and help Rushing Brook into Kaya's tepee. Kautsa follows and helps settle Little Branch on a sleeping mat. Then Kaya runs for the healer.

Bear Blanket arrives at the tepee in just a few moments and bends over to examine the baby. The healer straightens up. "Little Branch needs medicine," Bear Blanket says. She takes several small bundles from the pouch at her waist. "I have dried medicine here, but I need fresh juniper. It grows only on the flatlands. Someone must go and fetch some right away."

"We will go," Kaya volunteers. "We'll run as fast as deer, won't we, New Friend?"

"Yes!" I say, before I have a chance to think.

"Then hurry," Bear Blanket commands. "Her fever must not grow worse."

❖ *Turn to page 105.*

I don't want to get Squirrel into trouble, but I know there's nothing *I* can say to convince him to stop hurting the horse. So far, I haven't even been able to talk to Squirrel.

"Squirrel's done nothing but tease us since we arrived," I remind Kaya. "I'm not sure he will listen to you. But he'll listen to an elder. Toe-ta is here to help. He said he was."

Kaya considers this for a moment. Then she nods. "What you say is true about Squirrel. Let's go find Toe-ta."

We quickly make our way out of the bushes, leaving Squirrel where he is.

We find Toe-ta mounted on a powerful white stallion, who is dancing in a circle. Calmly, slowly, he brings the big horse to a stop and then pats his neck. "*Tawts*, my strong one! Soon, we'll run together." When he sees us, he says, "What is it, daughter?"

"Toe-ta, Squirrel needs your help with a horse. They're in those juniper trees." She points. Toe-ta's brow creases with concern and he quickly dismounts, handing the stallion's lead-rope to Jumps Back.

"What is happening here?" Toe-ta asks in his deep

voice as he pushes through the branches.

Squirrel is slapping the gray horse over and over with the rope. The horse is trying to rear now. At the sound of Toe-ta's voice, Squirrel's head snaps around, his eyes wide.

Toe-ta takes the lead-rope from Squirrel's hand. "*Nimíipuu* never strike an animal. We treat all creatures with respect."

Squirrel looks at the ground. "She wouldn't come," he mutters.

"Perhaps you were not asking in a way the horse could understand." He gazes down at the boy from his full height. "You were thinking about yourself, not this horse. Now return to the village. You will not be training horses anymore today."

Squirrel scowls stormily and pushes through the juniper without looking at Kaya or me. He leaves quickly, with no argument. I realize that I was half expecting him to talk back, the way Rachel did in the garden.

Toe-ta has no trouble gently leading the gray from the clearing, and we follow. "You and New Friend did what was best for the horse, daughter, even if Squirrel

had to learn a hard lesson. It was good that you asked for my help." He releases the gray into the clearing. "It's time to start some riding now."

"Yes, Toe-ta," Kaya answers. "Why don't you get on this one?" she says to me, patting a black-and-white-spotted horse.

I gulp. I'm going to ride the horse alone?

❖ *Turn to page 113.*

Crouching low, we dart through the grasses. Once we're out of sight of the clearing, we straighten up and run as fast as we can. On and on, our feet pound the hard-packed grass. I can feel my heart screaming in protest. The camp seems to be miles and miles away, but Kaya never slackens her speed. I fall behind, but Kaya runs swiftly, her feet barely seeming to touch the ground.

I'm on the verge of collapse when the sound of the falls grows louder and the pointed poles of the tepees appear on the horizon. I catch the scent of smoke from the fires. A few moments later, we burst into camp, covered in dust and panting. My heart is trying to pound its way out of my chest.

Brown Deer, Kautsa, and Speaking Rain are sitting near the tepee, weaving. Kautsa and Brown Deer jump to their feet as we run up. "Kaya! What is it?" Brown Deer gasps, her eyes wide and her hand on her chest.

Kaya tries to speak, but she's breathing too hard. She bends over with her hands on her knees, her back heaving. She gestures to the east. "Raiders . . . made off . . . with the herd."

"Quick!" Kautsa cries. "Brown Deer, tell the men!

They're down at the fishing platforms. Hurry!"

Brown Deer dashes down the path as quickly as her namesake, and moments later, several men run past us on their way out of camp.

"My little ones, you are so tired. Sit and rest." Kautsa dips a piece of soft buckskin in a bowl of water and wipes our faces. I close my eyes and let her gentle hands move from my forehead to my chin. Then it all hits me at once—everything that just happened—and I start shaking all over.

✦ *Turn to page 115.*

Kaya and I race up the path away from the falls. The roar of the water grows softer behind us, and the sun is hotter here. Kaya's pace is determined. We hurry, focused on our task, so I'm surprised when Kaya stops so suddenly that I almost bump into her.

"What is it?" I ask.

Kaya stands perfectly still. "Bear," she says in a low voice.

I stop, too. "Are there bears—"

"Hold still," Kaya whispers. "Do. Not. Move."

A bear is standing on the path, looking right at us.

My stomach drops. How can I hold still when every fiber of my being is telling me to run?

❖ *To follow your instincts and run,*
   turn to page 111.

❖ *To listen to Kaya and stay still,*
   turn to page 118.

K aya, I don't think—" I begin, but before I can say anything more, she bursts out from our hiding place.

"Squirrel, you're hurting that horse!" she exclaims. The boy's head whips around, and the horse snorts. "Stop!" Kaya demands.

I want to stay hidden. What will Squirrel say to Kaya's harsh words? But Kaya doesn't care. She stands with her hands on her hips, her eyes flashing and her hair blowing in the breeze. She looks as strong as an oak tree. Nothing scares her—and definitely not this boy.

"This mare won't follow me," Squirrel snaps. "Go away. I am working with her."

Kaya takes several purposeful, even breaths. Then she steps up and plucks the lead-rope from Squirrel's fingers. Sweat darkens the horse's face and neck. "You have to be a good leader if you expect a horse to follow you. You have to pay attention to what the horse needs, not just what you want."

Squirrel scowls at Kaya. He reaches out and takes the lead-rope from Kaya's hand. I tense up, watching. Is he going to hit the horse again?

"We will help you lead her back," Kaya offers.

Before Squirrel can react, Kaya positions herself on the other side of the gray horse's head. "Can you hold back the branches at the edge of the clearing?" she asks me. "I think she is uneasy about passing through them. That may have been what was keeping her from following you, Squirrel."

Kaya strokes the gray's cheek and runs her fingers under the rope halter, settling it back in place. "There now, are you ready to go back to the others?" she asks. Her voice is low and calm, as if she's having a conversation with a friend—which I guess she is. The gray horse drops her head and nuzzles Kaya's hand. "Don't be afraid. We will all help you," Kaya tells her.

I hold back the branches, and the gray follows Kaya and Squirrel tentatively out of the clearing, her ears pricked and her head high and wary.

Squirrel still doesn't say anything, but his face is no longer stormy. "*Katsee-yow-yow,*" he says, throwing us a backward glance before heading toward the herd.

Toe-ta greets Squirrel, and the two exchange a few words. When Toe-ta turns to Kaya with a questioning look on his face, she tells him we're going to take the

horse to the spring to cool her down. Toe-ta nods, and
he and Squirrel turn back to the herd.

I let my breath out in a huge rush. I'm impressed
that Kaya stood up to Squirrel, but I'm even more
impressed at what she said. Leaders *do* have to pay
attention to others. I don't think I've done that with
my garden group. "You helped that horse, Kaya,"
I say with admiration. "And you helped Squirrel, too.
I think you taught him something he needed to know."

"Toe-ta says that no one is born knowing about
horses," Kaya says thoughtfully as we make our way
away from the herd. "He says that it takes a lot of
patience to learn what we need to know."

"He's right," I say. *And not just about horses,* I think.
"You were very calm when you spoke to Squirrel."

"I used the breathing you showed me," she says
with a slight smile. "I was angry at Squirrel, but I did
not want my words to be harsh. You have taught me
something today."

❊ *Turn to page 129.*

Do it!" I say back. We have to take the risk.

Kaya lets out a low whistle, like the one she called Little Girl with before. The horse hears it! She pauses and turns toward our hiding place. Suddenly, a reddish horse crashes into her, and Little Girl stumbles. The other horse disappears again into the mass of plunging backs and tossing heads.

"She's hurt, Kaya!" I whisper. The filly is limping as she tries to trot away. But no one else notices her. The raiders drive away the last of the herd, and in a cloud of dust, Toe-ta and the others thunder after them.

Silence falls over the clearing. The herd site is utterly deserted—except for Little Girl, who stands alone, her chest heaving. Blood trickles from a gash on her leg.

I let out a big breath I didn't even realize I was holding. "What now?" We're alone, there are raiders somewhere out there, and the sun is already low in the sky.

Kaya is bending over Little Girl. Very gently, she runs her hands down the filly's leg. The horse jerks and trembles, but doesn't back away. "There now, precious one," she murmurs. "That hurts, doesn't it?" Kaya looks

up at me from her crouching position. "Nothing's broken, but she shouldn't walk all the way back to camp. Not without help."

I look around at the deepening shadows with an equally deepening sense of anxiety. "Are there any dangerous animals around here?" I ask.

Kaya nods. "Cougars. One of them could easily find Little Girl if we leave her to get help. Maybe we should wait with her until morning. Someone will be sure to come looking for us by then."

Stay out all night? I think to myself. Couldn't one of those cougars find *us* if we stay here? I wipe my now sweating palms on the sides of my dress.

❈ *To go back to camp for help,*
turn to page 125.

❈ *To stay with the filly,*
turn to page 120.

Despite Kaya's instructions, I can't hold still.

I turn and run back down the path. The bear growls, drops to all fours, and gives chase. I see a small tree ahead—one of the few trees around us. With a running leap, I grab a branch and heave myself up. The bear stands on its hind legs and tries to swipe at me. With a squeak, I pull my legs higher.

Suddenly, I think of Kaya. When I ran, I left her all alone. Will the bear turn and attack her instead? I shouldn't have left my friend!

I hear yelling behind me. Kaya is waving her arms and shrieking to distract the bear—to pull it away from me! But won't it lunge at her instead?

The bear glances around at the noise and takes another swipe at me. Then he drops to all fours. He doesn't seem to want to bother with us anymore. Snuffling the ground, he wanders off through the brush.

With my heart pounding its way out of my chest, I climb down from the tree and run to where Kaya is standing.

"I'm so sorry," I gasp. A few tears run down my cheeks. "I didn't listen to you, and the bear could have

killed us. It would've been my fault!" I thought only
of myself, even though Kaya rescued me—twice. Even
though she told me *Nimíipuu* always look out for one
another. Shame sits in my belly like a burning stone.

Kaya puts her arm around my shoulders. Her face
is troubled. "Perhaps you are still not well from your
fall," she says. "We need to get back to camp. Let's find
the juniper." Despite her kind words, I can see that
she's upset by my actions. I feel even worse knowing
that I've disappointed Kaya.

We find the juniper and hurry back to camp. My
heart is still pounding wildly in my chest, and I know
it's not just from the running.

❖ *Turn to page 122.*

I try to stall for time. I know I can't tell Kaya I've never ridden a horse before. She thinks I'm *Nimíipuu*, and *Nimíipuu* grow up riding horses. Kaya's looking at me expectantly.

"I don't know how well I'll ride alone today," I finally say, touching the scrape on my forehead.

"We will work slowly," Kaya assures me. "For both you and the horse."

Toe-ta strides over and steadies the horse. "Kaya is a strong rider," he says. "She will stay with you and help. I will, too."

Toe-ta's voice is kind, but my stomach twists in a nervous knot anyway. What if I mess up?

Kaya helps me mount the spotted horse. I clutch the mane with both hands until Toe-ta hands me the rope reins. Then I clutch those as well. The horse seems very big and very high now that I'm up here without Kaya. I can feel the power in his muscles, just barely concealed under his soft, shiny coat.

The horse tosses his head, and I grab more of the mane, giggling nervously. I grip his sides with my high leather moccasins, which helps.

"Lead him forward, Kaya," Toe-ta commands.

The horse steps forward at Kaya's request, and I lurch and almost plant my face in his mane. Quickly, I push myself up, hanging on to the reins. The horse jerks his head.

I turn to Toe-ta. His eyes are patient and kind. "What should I do when he jerks his head like that?" I finally ask.

"Relax your hands," Toe-ta says. "You'll be able to feel what he wants through the bit in his mouth."

I look down and see that I'm clutching the reins so hard, my knuckles are white. I loosen my fingers, and the horse drops his head a little, bobbing it up and down.

Toe-ta nods approval as Kaya leads us around and around. As I relax, I feel my abdomen moving with the horse's movement and I realize that I can feel the tension of the bit through the reins. When the horse stretches his neck out, I can feel the reins tighten. And when he brings his neck back a little, I can feel them slacken.

"Now, New Friend on her own!" Toe-ta calls.

◈ *Turn to page 126.*

You're trembling," Eetsa says quietly as she kneels between Kaya and me. She hands us each a horn cup of cold water. My feet burn, and the muscles in my legs give little pops and twitches as I try to rest. But the pain in my limbs is nothing compared with the pain in my heart. What will happen to Kaya's father and uncle? What will happen to the horses? Will Little Girl be safe?

Kautsa gives me a wooden bowl of hot salmon broth, and I clutch it, drawing strength from its warmth. "Our warriors will get the herd back," she says.

Slowly, Kaya and I sip the hot broth. It feels good to sit here quietly, the nourishing liquid spreading comfort through my shaking body. I'm not a fan of fish, but I'm thankful for it now. When I finally put down the bowl, my belly is full and my shaking has stopped. Speaking Rain combs out my braids and plaits them smooth again. Long Legs pads up to Kaya and leans against her side. She rubs his ears and for a minute lays her head on his back. When she sits up, the dog meanders over to me. He drops to his belly and puts his head in my lap.

At first, I shrink back from the dog. But then
I remember what Kaya said about listening to animals.
Is this dog trying to comfort me? I touch his head. Long
Legs's fur is thick and warm. Over and over, I stroke
him. His ears are as soft as the lamb's ears I grow in
my garden. I think of the soft silvery-green plants in
a bank by the fence. Dad and I planted them together.
I swallow hard, sudden tears pricking my eyes. I wish
Dad were here now—or I were home. And where are
Toe-ta and Jumps Back? Why is there no news? I lower
my head and swipe my hand across the back of my
eyes.

Kaya picks up a half-finished basket nearby and
begins to weave as the sun drops lower and lower in
the sky. But she fumbles with the grasses, and the
basket tumbles to the ground.

Kautsa picks it up and sets it aside. "Did I ever tell
you that *Nimíipuu* didn't have any horses when I was
a girl?" She settles herself close to us.

Her steady voice is like a calming tonic. Kaya must
feel the same way because she smiles for the first time
since the raid. "That was a long time ago," she says.

"Aa-heh, it was! We traveled everywhere on foot."

Kautsa's eyes are distant with remembering. "Our dogs were big and strong and pulled our heavy loads for us. Our scouts were as swift as antelope when they ran to warn us of danger."

I have no trouble believing that, given how fast Kaya ran all the way back from the clearing.

"We ride faster and farther now," Kautsa goes on, "but our warriors must fight to protect the horses—as they are doing now."

The shadows are growing long and the sun is just a pink streak in the western sky when the hoofbeats of a galloping horse make us all look up.

❖ *Turn to page 132.*

hough my mind is screaming "run!" I muster my strength and do as Kaya tells me. We hold perfectly still. "Don't look at him," Kaya mutters out of the corner of her mouth. I stare at the ground, my body frozen. The bear is huge, and I feel very small and completely unprotected.

The bear snuffles the ground, grunting moistly. I can smell him—a thick, musky odor of fur and mud. My heart pounds in my ears so loud I fear the bear can hear it. A droplet of sweat runs down my cheek, but I don't dare move to wipe it off. I keep my eyes fixed on the path, where I can see the bear's legs but nothing else.

Beside me, Kaya is as still as a stick. *Please, please, please,* my mind pleads. The bear shuffles off the path. I don't dare breathe. He stops to sniff a bush. Then I sense him turning his head. I raise my eyes the tiniest fraction. He gives us one last stare and then waddles off through the brush.

I let out the breath I've been holding. My knees are wobbling, and I feel like I could cry. I turn to Kaya, who looks much calmer than I feel. I realize that this isn't the first time she's encountered a bear.

"He wanted berries," Kaya says. "We just happened to be in his path." Kaya turns and waves me on. "We need to find the juniper."

I hurry after her. I'd almost forgotten about the juniper! "Does that kind of thing happen often?"

Kaya nods. "At this time of year, the bears are hungry and searching for food."

I'm still shaking, but I try to channel some of Kaya's calm acceptance by taking deep breaths. After a few minutes, my knees are steadier.

"This way," Kaya says. "We must find the juniper and hurry back to Little Branch."

❖ *Turn to page 133.*

aybe she can walk if we lead her," I suggest. But the filly stumbles when she tries to take just a few steps. There's no way she can make it back to camp. She looks so small and forlorn, I can't stand the idea of leaving her. "We need to stay with her," I tell Kaya.

Kaya looks at the rapidly setting sun, then at the open land around us. *"Aa-heh,"* she agrees. "It's the only way we'll be sure she'll survive the night."

The wind blows and I shiver. The land around us feels so big and empty that I begin to regret my decision.

But I see the determination in Kaya's eyes. I know this is the right thing to do for Little Girl. I'm just not sure how *this* girl is going to manage.

"The first thing we need is a fire," Kaya says. "It will give us warmth and light, and keep away the wolves."

I gulp. Did she say *wolves*?

Kaya takes a small bone knife from her pouch. Expertly, she sharpens a stick and gathers a pile of crushed dried leaves. It takes me a minute to realize that she's going to build a fire—without a single match in sight. She rapidly spins the point of the stick in a hole in another branch. After a few moments, little puffs of smoke rise around the sticks. Then a tiny flame appears in the leaves. I'm glad the darkening twilight hides the surprise on my face.

"What can I do to help?" I say somewhat weakly.

"We need some yarrow leaves for a poultice to treat Little Girl's leg," Kaya says. "But it will be difficult to find them in the dark."

"Oh, I can find them," I say, relieved to finally feel confident about something. *I can't start a fire, but I can find a yarrow leaf,* I think as I search within the circle of the fire's glow.

I recognize the fine, feathery leaves, and the lacy white flowers show up well in the fire's dancing light. "*Tawts,*" Kaya says when I return with the leaves in my hand. "Now let's build a shelter before it's completely dark."

Build a shelter? From what?

◈ *Turn to page 142.*

We have it!" Kaya cries as we enter the tepee.

Little Branch's face is still red and flushed with fever. She lies limply in her mother's lap, her head dangling over Rushing Brook's arm. Her little body is utterly still except for the quick rise and fall of her chest.

"*Tawts.*" Bear Blanket quickly takes the juniper and dunks it in a small basket of hot water that is waiting beside the fire.

Kaya smooths the baby's forehead. "Don't worry, precious one. This good medicine will make you better."

But the baby doesn't move, and Rushing Brook cradles her closer. The young mother looks at Bear Blanket with fear in her eyes.

The healer dips out a small cup of the hot tea and sets it beside Rushing Brook. "We must wait for it to cool," she murmurs and sits back on her heels.

Rushing Brook utters a little groan and drops her head to her baby again. I can see that waiting for the medicine is agony for her—and it is for Kaya and me, too. My own fingers are knotted in my lap, and Kaya is fidgeting with impatience beside me. Even Kautsa looks worried. Only Bear Blanket is calm, her hand quiet on her knees, her gaze fixed steadily on the tepee wall. I flash on what Kaya told me earlier: that Bear Blanket keeps her mind clean so that she is ready to help. Perhaps that is why she is so patient.

After several minutes, Bear Blanket cradles Little Branch's downy head with her strong, wrinkled hand. She tips small sips of tea into the baby's mouth. Drop by drop, the baby swallows the tea until finally Bear Blanket takes the cup from her lips. "*Tawts*," she says. "We must wait and let the medicine do its work."

"Will she be well?" Rushing Brook begs. Tears glisten in the corners of her eyes, and I feel my own eyes well up with sympathy. The baby has to get better! She just has to!

Bear Blanket lays a hand on the young mother's shoulder. "Let's take her out into the air. The breezes will cool her cheeks. Then we will wait. That is what we can do now."

As she and Rushing Brook make their way out of the tepee, I rub my hand across my eyes. It seems as if this day has lasted for weeks. I'm worn out.

"Lie down," Kautsa tells me. "You are still unwell."

Kautsa helps me onto her deerskin, and then softly she and Kaya slip out of the tepee.

I close my weary eyes, but my mind won't let me rest. I can't stop thinking about what happened with the bear. I wish I hadn't run when Kaya told me not to. I wish I hadn't let my friend down. But coming face-to-face with an actual bear was really scary. Kaya may be used to dealing with wild animals, but I'm not. We were in serious danger. Even with Kaya's help, I'm not sure I want to face another bear—or anything else that's living outside Kaya's tepee. This particular adventure is more than I can handle right now. I look at my bracelet. Maybe it's time for me to go home.

After an hour of not sleeping, I get up and lift the tepee flap. Bear Blanket and Kautsa are talking softly. "How is Little Branch?" I ask.

"See for yourself," Rushing Brook answers.

❖ *Turn to page 135.*

aya, I think we should go back to camp and get help," I say. "Besides, your mother will be worried about you soon." I think of how my own mom would panic if I wasn't home by dark.

Kaya nods. She looks deep into the horse's eyes, stroking her face. "Little Girl, I don't want to leave you," she says. The horse snuffles and leans her head against Kaya. They're talking to each other again.

Then Kaya straightens up. "Let's run for help. It's a risk, but we'll try. We have to trust that she'll be all right."

I nod. We lead the horse slowly to the side of the clearing where there's some long grass. She can rest there and eat until we return. Kaya plucks a handful of the grass and twists it into a soft wisp. Gently, she binds it around Little Girl's leg like a bandage. Meanwhile, I clear away some broken branches from the grassy spot so that she'll have a comfortable place to lie down.

Kaya strokes the filly's black nose. "We'll be back, little one. Have courage."

❖ *Turn to page 137.*

aya lets go of the horse's halter and steps back. The horse shakes his head a little but keeps walking slowly and steadily. I expect to be scared without Kaya's help, but I discover that I'm not. I sit tall, carrying the reins easily between my fingers. I'm doing it! I'm riding a horse!

Then, as we pass a cluster of stones, the horse jumps a little, throwing his head up at the same time. I yelp, my face almost colliding with his neck, and slide to one side. "Sit up!" Kaya calls out, and quickly I wriggle back to the middle.

"Easy, boy," I murmur to the horse, and he settles back to his walk. A flush of pride sweeps over me. I didn't fall off—and I calmed the horse!

"You did well," Toe-ta says, and I grin. I reach down and give my horse a firm pat on the shoulder.

We parade around the clearing several more times. With each step, I can feel my back stretching taller and my legs relaxing.

"Your horse is learning quickly," Toe-ta says. "Now Kaya will ride, and you can lead."

I gently pull back on the reins, and to my delight, the horse stops immediately. I lean into his neck and

swing my leg over, sliding to the ground. I stumble and almost fall, but catch myself just in time.

Then Kaya hands me the lead-rope and swings onto the horse's back. "I'm ready!" she calls.

I loop the lead-rope in my hand. The horse blows his breath out with a whoosh. I jump and then steady myself. I cluck to him, as I've heard Kaya do, and he starts walking beside me. I feel his hot breath on my hand. His big hooves raise puffs of dust with each step. Somehow, he seems even more powerful now that I'm on the ground beside him. After all, he's still a wild animal, I remind myself. He could knock me to the ground with one bump of his head. But his long-lashed eyes are bright and curious. He wants to work with us, just as we want to work with him.

After a few more times around, Toe-ta tells us it's time we head back to camp.

"*Katsee-yow-yow,*" I tell the horse, stroking his soft nose.

Kaya dismounts and smiles at me. "You did well, working with this young colt."

"You're a good teacher," I respond.

"You have both done good work today," Toe-ta tells

us, swinging onto his stallion. "You helped each other, and you helped the horses trust you."

Neither of us can conceal our smiles at his praise.

"Do you want to ride back on the chestnut alone?" Kaya offers. "I'll ride with Toe-ta."

This time, I agree eagerly. As we head back to camp, my horse begins trotting, moving faster. I lift my face into the sweet, grass-scented breeze and let the wind blow back my braids. I've never felt so free—and so brave. Horses don't seem quite as scary now. I've learned to mount and ride a horse by myself. I've spent all day outside, getting tired and dirty. I feel almost as if it was a different girl—a smaller, more timid me—that landed on the riverbank earlier today.

◈ *Turn to page 53.*

The horse is still agitated from her ordeal, and she trots a few steps, turning her head to the side. She shies, jumping a little at a stray leaf blowing in front of her, and Kaya instinctively moves her body closer to the horse. "There now. It's just a leaf," she says, her voice low and soothing. She stops the horse, and we stand for a long time as Kaya strokes her nose, then her ears, over and over until her head drops and her muscles relax. When we start walking again, the horse follows us easily.

After a few minutes of walking, we arrive at a burbling stream that winds its way through the grasses, chuckling quietly to itself as it flows over smooth brown stones. The gray horse dips her head to the water, snuffling and blowing as she drinks. Kaya tugs off her moccasins and dangles her legs in the water. "Join me," she says, patting the grass beside her.

I sit and slowly unwind the laces from my moccasins. I'm still nervous about snakes and anything else that might be living in the stream. But I'm hot and tired, and Kaya looks pretty comfortable on the edge of the stream. I tentatively dip my feet in the water. It's cold, but wonderfully refreshing. And nothing has slithered past me—yet.

"Do you remember the story about how *Nimíipuu* got their horses?" Kaya asks, dabbling her foot up and down in the sparkling water.

Wait. Haven't Nimíipuu always had horses? I wonder. "I may have forgotten," I say. "Would you tell me?"

"*Aa-heh,*" she says with a smile. I can tell that Kaya is happy to tell the story. Anything with horses makes her happy.

"Many, many winters ago," Kaya begins, "before our grandmothers and their grandmothers were born, a ship came, with pale, hairy men on it. The ship stopped near the shore and from the ship, three stallions came swimming through the water. *Nimíipuu* traders watched these beautiful creatures climb up onto the beach and shake the water from their long manes and silvery white bodies. *Nimíipuu* received them with awe. The stallions had powerful medicine in their spirits. They traveled with the traders back to the *Nimíipuu* camp, and there they were bred to the mares. The foals born from these stallions had that powerful medicine in them, too. These stallions are the fathers of the horses we have now, and over the years, The People came to call them the Ghost Wind Stallions," Kaya finishes.

"The Ghost Wind Stallions!" I whisper with awe. I look down at my feet, distorted through the surface of the water. I think of the traders watching those strong stallions climbing out of the water onto the beach. My throat swells unexpectedly at the beauty of the image. And now the children of those first horses are here, still with their *Nimíipuu* family. I can see now how important horses are to Kaya's people—and why Kaya loves them so much.

"It's time to go back to Toe-ta," Kaya says, and I pull my thoughts back to the present. We pull our feet out, drying them on the tall grass. As we walk back to the herd, Kaya loops her arm through mine and we match our steps together, with the gray horse walking beside us. But when we top the last small rise and look down at the clearing where the herd was grazing, we see only mashed grass and bare spots. Toe-ta, the other riders, and the herd are gone!

❧ *Turn to page 138.*

Raven pounds into camp a moment later and swings off his sweat-streaked horse. "The herd is safe," he says in response to our questioning faces. "Our men were able to catch up and drive the enemies off. They are on their way back now."

There are murmurs of relief. Kaya's family is safe!

"Did you see a little black-and-white horse in the herd?" Kaya asks, groping for my hand. "She has a white patch on her forehead."

"I don't know . . ." Raven frowns, and my stomach plunges. Did Little Girl get lost in the crush? Did she wander off alone, maybe hurt?

Kaya squeezes my hand harder, the color draining from her cheeks. I squeeze her hand back and hold my breath, waiting for Raven's answer.

Then Raven's brow clears. *"Aa-heh!"* he says. "There is a filly with the herd. I remember the white patch on her forehead."

I let my breath out in a great rush. Kaya relaxes her grip on my fingers. Little Girl is safe! Today's adventure has ended well. Now it's time for me to go home.

※ *Turn to page 149.*

The juniper is right around here," Kaya says a few minutes later. We leave the path and wade through a jumble of grasses and plants. I see sagebrush, tall clumps of dry grass, thorny tangles of wild rose-bushes, and—

"Kaya, stop!"

She freezes. "What is it?"

I point to a low shrub with shiny leaves. "Poison oak! You almost stepped in it."

"I didn't see it—*katsee-yow-yow*!" Kaya says. "You have a good eye for plants, New Friend."

I nod, saying, "Here's the juniper—how much do we need?"

We break off several small branches, tuck them into our waist pouches, and hurry back to the falls.

Back at the camp, we dash into Kaya's tepee. Little Branch is lying still in Rushing Brook's lap, her face obscured by the blanket her mother holds closely around her.

"*Tawts!* You found the juniper!" Bear Blanket exclaims.

"New Friend found it," Kaya says.

"We are grateful," Bear Blanket says.

Kautsa drops hot stones into a basket of water and Bear Blanket adds the juniper, stirring it until the water is a light green. Bear Blanket fills a small horn cup, and we all wait while she blows on the tea to cool it. After several long minutes, Bear Blanket tips a few drops into the baby's mouth. The child cries out weakly, and Rushing Brook looks up at the healer with desperation.

Bear Blanket steadies the baby's chin and pours in a little more of the juniper brew. "There now, little one," she murmurs. The baby trembles. For a minute, her body goes stiff. I gasp and clutch Kaya's hand. Then the baby relaxes. Bear Blanket mutters something to herself and shakes her head. I see Kautsa's lips tighten as if she's worried.

I look at Kaya, who is focused on Little Branch. Neither of us can move from the baby's side. We have to know if the medicine will work.

❖ *Turn to page 139.*

I peer over the loosely wrapped bundle in Running Brook's arms and exhale at the sight of the tiny face peacefully sleeping. I touch her forehead. Her skin is cool and damp.

"The medicine you brought has helped her, young visitor," Bear Blanket says.

"Go tell Kaya," Kautsa says. "She is getting water at the stream."

I run down the path to the stream. My happiness at the baby's recovery mingles with the heaviness from the bear encounter and the sadness at what I know I must do now.

I find Kaya just rising from the bank of the stream, a water basket in her arms.

"Little Branch is better," I tell her.

Her face lights up with a smile. "*Tawts!*" Then her brow creases as she looks at me more closely. "Something else is wrong. I can see that you are troubled."

"Kaya, that bear scared me," I confess.

"*Aa-heh,*" she says gently. "Next time, you must remember to stay calm and quiet."

"The bear made me think of how scared I was when

I almost fell into the river. It's time for me to go to my family. I remember where to find them now."

Kaya's round face crinkles with concern. "I should go with you."

"No, no," I assure her. "You've already done so much for me. I will be safe. I promise." Kaya nods. I reach out and squeeze her hand, trying to keep back the tears that threaten to fall at any moment.

"Remember," Kaya says. "Mistakes are not bad. They teach us to do better next time." She smiles as she echoes Kautsa's words and holds my hand a moment longer. "I hope to see you again, my friend."

"I hope so, too," I say.

I watch Kaya walk up the path toward the camp, her long braids swaying with her steps. When she is out of sight, I glance around to make sure I'm alone. Then I trace my finger around the shell. In an instant, I'm whirled back to my own world.

❖ *Turn to page 47.*

The sun has almost disappeared from the horizon, and the sky is a soft purple. Darkness is beginning to gather under the bushes and trees. I look back at Little Girl, lying down in the grass where we left her. She looks vulnerable, and I wish there were more we could do for her.

Kaya and I run toward the river and the safety of camp. But the distance seems a lot longer on foot, and the night is growing dimmer and colder by the minute. Shadows surround me, and the grass rustles against us. The dusk seems so much bigger out here than at home near my house. I'm chilly and clammy, and my feet hurt from stumbling against the tough hillocks of grass. Kaya keeps up a steady pace. Are we going to run the entire way back to camp? I'm dying for a rest, but it seems wimpy to ask. Instead, I try to focus ahead of me, scanning the horizon for any sign of the camp. Nothing—just vast blackness. Just then, a howl comes from somewhere in the dark, and my heart gives a big thump.

❖ *Turn to page 147.*

aya and I look at each other in astonishment.
"Where did they go?" I ask.

Kaya shakes her head. "I don't know. Surely Toe-ta would have come for us if they were going to move the horses."

We stand in the middle of the dusty clearing and silence falls around us, broken only by the whisper of the wind in the grasses and the quiet snuffles of the gray horse. My skin crawls suddenly. There's an eerie feeling in the empty space.

"Kaya, what are we going to do?"

Her usually cheerful face is sober. "Let's go back to camp. Maybe Toe-ta has returned there as well."

I hug myself with my arms, and a pang of home-sickness stabs me in my throat. All of a sudden I want my own dad to give me a hug and make me feel safe. But he's most definitely not here and neither is Toe-ta. Kaya and I are alone.

◈ *Turn to page 157.*

We wait quietly. Outside, we hear footsteps, talking, and laughter as people walk past the tepee. Eventually I can tell by the silence outside that the camp is mostly empty.

Bear Blanket feels the baby's chest and hands. "The fever is falling," she finally announces. We all breathe a deep sigh of relief. "But she needs to be watched," the healer continues, "and Rushing Brook must rest."

"Kaya and I will stay with the baby," I say. I've spent enough time with Kaya's people to understand how important it is to care for others. I don't want to miss the festivities, but I feel good about the decision. I think Kaya feels good too, because she smiles at me and squeezes my hand.

"*Aa-heh*, we'll stay," she echoes.

Kautsa gives us an approving nod, and she and Bear Blanket leave the tepee. Kaya prepares a sleeping mat for Rushing Brook, who lies down and is asleep almost immediately.

Kaya cradles the baby in her lap. "Are you sorry to miss the festivities?" Kaya asks me, wrapping the rabbit skin closely around the baby.

"I am," I reply, tracing the baby's little eyebrows

with the tip of one finger. "But *Nimíipuu* always look out for one another," I say, repeating Kautsa's words.

Kaya nods seriously. "That's true. We are like wolves—strong as individuals but even stronger when we all work together."

I shudder at the mention of wolves. I think one wild animal encounter is enough for my time with Kaya.

The sun's evening rays make slow patterns through the tepee cracks. The baby sleeps and stirs, then sleeps again. Then she wakes with a little cry. Kaya feels her forehead. "Still warm," she says, keeping her voice low. "She's probably wet, too."

"Should we dry her?" I ask. Kaya's people don't have diapers, I'm guessing, not that I'd know what to do if they did. I haven't done much diaper changing in my life.

"*Aa-heh*," Kaya says. She unwraps the baby from the blanket. Little Branch has buckskin wrapped around her feet and legs. Kaya unties the lacing holding it together and pulls it away. There's no diaper under-neath. Instead, Rushing Brook has cushioned her baby's bottom with some kind of fluffy shredded plant.

"This cattail fluff is soaked," Kaya says, pulling it

away. She wipes Little Branch and plucks some dry fluff from a small bag nearby. She puts the fluff under the baby and wraps her up again.

That was definitely not like any diaper I've ever seen. But it seems to do the job because the baby is cooing and waving her fists.

Rushing Brook is awake now. She gets up and comes over to feel her baby's forehead. "Damp and cool," she says. "Bear Blanket's medicine is good."

I feel like cheering, but I settle for kissing the baby on the forehead.

"You two go on to the festivities," Rushing Brook urges us. "My baby and I will be well here."

"*Aa-heh*, we'll go, if you are sure you are rested," Kaya says. Rushing Brook nods. We jump up and then kiss the baby one more time.

Kautsa is outside, and we tell her that the baby's fever has broken. Kautsa smiles. "Now it is time for us to join the others at the feast," she says.

✤ *Turn to page 23.*

I wet the leaves with water from Kaya's drinking pouch and wrap them around the filly's injured leg. Kaya secures them with a piece of fringe from her dress. Then she quickly cuts a handful of branches from the nearby trees and arranges them into a tent-like shelter that's just big enough for the two of us to crawl into and lie down. The sky turns red-gold, then light purple, then deeper purple, and the first stars wink at us. Then eerie yapping howls arise from somewhere not far away.

"Wh-what is that?" I ask, unable to keep the quiver out of my voice.

"Just coyotes," Kaya reassures me. "They won't bother us."

She cuts more branches and builds up the fire, and we settle in front of it. The filly lies nearby. Kaya opens her pouch and hands me a piece of pemmican. When we were making fresh pemmican ealier, I didn't want to try it. But now I'm hungry, so I take a tiny bite. It tastes like fish, which I'm not crazy about. But I'm glad to have something to eat.

Kaya's made us a little home here, I think, as I place my feet close to the fire to warm them. We had noth-

ing, and Kaya built us a house and a fire and we have some food—all from the things around us. All this earth and these plants and animals are Kaya's home.

The filly snuffles and sighs near the shelter. Kaya and I watch the fire burn down to coals. When we crawl into our shelter to sleep, I don't feel quite as frightened as I thought I'd be out here in the dark.

❈ *Turn to page 153.*

After all the food has been served, we sit down on the floor to begin eating. I look around eagerly for the fry bread. That's what I remember from the modern pow-wow at Wallowa. The deep-fried dough covered with butter and sugar is delicious. Thinking of the hot, crisp bread makes my stomach rumble. I realize I haven't eaten in hours, and I'm famished. I don't see any bread, but Kaya offers me something that looks like a sweet potato.

"It's camas root," she gently reminds me.

It looks strange, but Kaya's watching me, so I take a tentative bite. There's no salt or butter or spices on it, but it's surprisingly sweet—almost like a pear. It probably won't ever be my favorite food, but at least I can say I tried it.

When an old woman offers me some salmon, I know I can't refuse. Everyone is grateful for the fresh fish, and now I understand how hard the men worked to catch it and how much time the women spent to prepare it. I've never tried salmon before, so I take a tiny bite, expecting it to be kind of slimy. It's really not that bad—it has a smoky flavor from the fires, and it doesn't taste fishy the way some fish does. It's not what

I'm used to, but then again, nothing in Kaya's world is what I'm used to.

I'm relieved when someone passes me a small bowl of dried huckleberries. At least I know what these are. Lily and I always pick them off the bushes that grow at the edge of her yard. I scoop the sweet berries into my mouth. They're shriveled like raisins, but the taste is still familiar.

After we eat, Kaya and I follow the crowd outside. Everyone is laughing and talking happily. The drumming is louder out here, and we're all drawn in the direction of the sound.

"Look!" Kaya cries. "A horse race is starting." She points to a long, flat spot in the distance. Riders are lining up, and their beautiful horses toss their heads and nicker with excitement.

A burst of laughter behind us makes me turn. There's a group of girls talking excitedly, each showing off a different item—a flat woven bag, a doll, a white bone bead like the ones in the necklace I made earlier today. One girl even has a gray puppy under her arm.

"I'll give you this gathering bag for your doll," the girl with the bag says. The other one nods eagerly, and they exchange the items. They're trading!

One of the horses lining up for the race lets out a loud whinny. "Should we go watch the race?" Kaya asks. "Or should we join the girls who are trading?"

◈ *To join the trading,*
   turn to page 151.

◈ *To go see the horse race,*
   go online to **beforever.com/endings**

※••••※••••※••••※••◆•••※••••※••••※••••※

as that a wolf?" I pant as we run.

"A coyote," Kaya says.

I'm hopeful when I hear the sound of the falls, faint at first, and then louder. Finally, I spot some small orange lights ahead—the campfires of the village! Panting, we stumble into camp. Kautsa and Eetsa jump up when they see us, and Speaking Rain and Brown Deer crowd around. A tall older man emerges from the tepee. "We have been worried about you, granddaughter," he says. He must be Kaya's grandfather.

Gasping for breath, our words tumbling over each other's, we explain about the raid and the injured filly. "Toe-ta and the others rode off after the herd. We need to go back, Pi-lah-ka," Kaya says to her grandfather. "We need to bring Little Girl back to camp, but we need help."

"No one is going anywhere tonight," Pi-lah-ka answers. "It is dark, and danger is still out there. We will go in the morning." His voice is firm.

Kaya and I look at each other and swallow our disappointment. We can't argue with Pi-lah-ka, of course. Kautsa wraps us in warm buckskin cloaks and feeds us bowls of boiled salmon. Fish isn't really my

favorite, but this has a delicious smoky flavor. I eat it all, realizing how hungry I am. When I set the bowl down, I think about Mom and Dad. I feel as if I haven't seen them for a long, long time. A wave of longing for my own family washes over me, and my fingers stray to my bracelet. But I can't leave until I know that Kaya's family and Little Girl are safe.

Later, I lie under a rabbit-skin blanket in the tepee next to Kaya. My belly is comfortably full, though my legs ache and my feet feel as though they've been pounded flat from all the running. The heat from the fire warms my face. All around me are the little rustles and murmurs from the rest of Kaya's sleeping family. But I can't sleep. I can't stop thinking about Little Girl and wondering if Toe-ta is safe. I stare at the fire for a long time before I finally give in to my weariness.

❈ *Turn to page 160.*

aya claps her hands and jumps to her feet.

"Let's go out to meet them!"

I rise to my feet, my whole body aching. My muscles feel like rubber bands that have been stretched too far, from working with horses, the long run back to camp, and the strain of waiting for the news. I've never wanted a hot bath more badly in my life, and now that I have started thinking about home, it's hard to stop. I want to see Mom and Dad.

"Kaya, wait," I say. "I remember now where I was going when we met on the riverbank. I'm ready to go back to my own camp." I put my hand on her shoulder. "Thank you for everything you've shown me today. I'll never forget it." I feel like I've never spoken truer words.

Kaya nods. "I'll miss you. But I am glad you are going to your family."

I look at Kaya's family and feel a rush of gratitude for everything they've done for me today. "*Katsee-yow-yow* for caring for me," I say. *Thank you for showing me how beautiful your homeland is,* I add silently. *Thank you for showing me how beautiful nature can be. Thank you for showing me how brave I can be.* "Bear Blanket was right.

I've found what I was seeking. I'm ready to go on with my journey now."

Kaya walks me down the path toward the river-bank. "Will you be able to make your way across the river?" she asks.

"I will," I say. "I promise. Please don't worry."

We both linger, not wanting to say good-bye. "I will miss you, New Friend," Kaya sighs.

I take her hands in mine. "I'm going to miss you, too. But don't forget Little Girl. She's waiting for you." I feel happier thinking of Kaya and Little Girl reunited.

A smile lifts Kaya's face. "And your family is waiting for you."

Halfway down the path to the river, I stop and look back at Kaya. She waves at me as the wind dances the fringe on her dress.

❁ *Turn to page 165.*

I can't resist getting a closer look at the things the girls are trading, so I step toward the group. But Kaya stops me, her face bright with an idea. "You and I could be trading partners! Then we'll be friends for as long as we live. What do you think?"

"Yes!" I say right away. "Of course we'll be friends forever."

Kaya's whole face lights up. She puts her hands behind her neck and unties the colorful quill necklace she's wearing. "Here. I want you to have this. Kautsa made it for me when I was a very small girl."

I inhale as I run my fingers over the lovely smooth quills. "Thank you," I breathe. But what do I have to offer Kaya in return? I think about the pink stone I found on the hillside, but I remember what Kaya said: *For a good trade, you have to offer something of equal value in return.* The stone is not a good enough trade—not for someone who saved my life! I don't have anything.

Except my bracelet.

I remember how Kaya admired it. And it *is* special. Of course, it's my only link to home. But couldn't I borrow the bracelet when I'm ready to go home? On the other hand, it seems risky to let the bracelet out of

my sight. But what if I don't trade the bracelet to Kaya? Maybe that's what trading partners are supposed to do.

◈ *To trade your bracelet to Kaya,*
   turn to page 155.

◈ *To keep your bracelet,*
   go to page 164.

In the morning, we're awakened by two scouts searching for us. They have good news. Raven has just arrived back at the camp with word that the herd is safe, along with all the *Nimíipuu* warriors. Kaya and I both breathe a big sigh of relief.

Little Girl is better after a night of rest. She's walking with less of a limp, and the scouts are sure that, if we go slowly, the filly can make it back to camp.

Kaya puts a lead-rope around Little Girl's neck, and the three of us walk unhurriedly behind the scouts' horses. The morning air is fresh, and I watch swallows dip and dive in the clear sky above us.

"I thought of something last night," Kaya says. "I will ask Toe-ta if I can keep Little Girl and train her myself. When her injury heals, I'll call her Steps High."

"Because that's what she'll do again one day," I finish. "That's the perfect name."

I'm filled with inspiration this morning, too. I can't wait to get home and call Lily. She'll be so excited when she hears I'm ready for camp. And then I'll go tackle my garden group. I've survived a raid, taken care of an injured horse, and spent the night out in the open. The garden project doesn't seem nearly as difficult now.

I can stand up to Rachel and Sarah.

I look at Kaya gently leading Little Girl home. Will Kaya ever know how much she's taught me? About courage? About resourcefulness? *Katsee-yow-yow, my friend*, I tell her in my mind. *Katsee-yow-yow.*

❖ *The End* ❖

To read this story another way and see how different choices lead to a different ending, turn back to page 52.

I look deep into my friend's eyes. "Kaya, I want to trade you my bracelet. It's the most special piece of jewelry I have. I want my most special friend to have it." I untie the bracelet from my own wrist and fasten it around Kaya's.

"*Katsee-yow-yow!*" She lifts her wrist and studies the bracelet, delight on her face.

I have a sense of being set adrift, like a balloon with its string cut, floating up and away—away from the chance to return to my own time.

Another girl about our age wanders over. She speaks to Kaya using the sign language that Kaya calls "throwing words." She's gesturing to the bracelet, smiling, and Kaya nods and smiles back, signing her reply.

"Kaya, what's she saying?" I ask with more than a touch of anxiety.

"She says she's never seen a bracelet like this before," Kaya tells me. "She wants to know where I got it. I told her my trading partner wove it. We both agree that it's beautiful."

Kaya's words make me feel warm all over. But then the girl picks up a chubby, fuzzy little puppy

tumbling at her feet. She throws some more words to Kaya, points to my bracelet, and holds out the pup, who whines and tries to lick Kaya's face. I don't need to throw words to understand what she wants—to trade my bracelet for the puppy!

The bottom drops out of my stomach. I've seen how much Kaya loves dogs. Would she trade my bracelet away?

◈ *Turn to page 162.*

We mount the gray horse double and begin the ride back to camp. My legs and arms ache from the day's work, and the jostling of the horse seems endless. Thoughts of my parents and my own home keep swimming up to the top of my mind.

Finally, I hear the falls begin to roar and see the spiky tops of the tepees. We're nearing camp!

We leave the gray horse in the pasture at the top of the flatland. Kaya says she doesn't see Toe-ta's stallion, but there are many horses, and we don't search for long. As we walk into the camp, Long Legs barks a greeting, and Brown Deer calls Kaya's name. Speaking Rain jumps to her feet, her partly finished basket tumbling from her lap. "I was so worried about you, sister!" she cries. Eetsa comes forward with outstretched arms.

"What's wrong?" Kaya asks in confusion.

"You are safe," Eetsa breathes. She lays her hand against Kaya's cheek, and I swallow hard against the lump that has risen in my throat. That's just what my own mom does. I wish I could feel her touch now.

Then we spot Raven sitting nearby. Kautsa bends over him. He's covered with dust and his braids are

mussed. A long scratch trickles blood down his cheek.

"What happened, Raven?" Kaya kneels beside him.

He winces a little as Kautsa dabs at his cheek with a piece of buckskin. "Enemy raiders from the plains crept up on us after you two went to the spring. We didn't see them until they had surrounded us. Two of them held us back with arrows while the rest made off with the herd. They're headed for the hills. Toe-ta and Jumps Back went after them. They told me to run to the stream to get you and then come back here to send the other warriors. But I couldn't find you at the stream— I must have gone to the wrong watering place. I ran back here as fast as I could."

Kaya and I stare at each other wide-eyed. We just missed a raid!

"You are fortunate, girls," Kautsa says. "Had you been there when the raiders attacked, they could have carried you off, too."

My heart gives a quick double-thump. Carried off by raiders and then . . . what? I check to make sure my bracelet—my link to home—is still on my wrist. It is. I feel shaky suddenly and sink down gratefully on the mat Brown Deer spreads for me.

"I'm worried about Toe-ta and Jumps Back." Kaya looks almost on the verge of tears. She bites her lip.

Kautsa lays her hand on Kaya's shoulder. "Your father and uncle are strong and courageous warriors," she says firmly. "They will be back, with the horses."

Kaya nods and I can see that the conviction in Kautsa's voice has soothed her—a little.

❈ *Turn to page 169.*

It is morning! We are alive!" A voice filters through my dreams. I open my eyes. Morning light streams into the tepee, and outside the door, a man calls out to the camp, "The sun is witness to what we do today!"

Beside me, Kaya sits up. "I hope the sun is witness to our finding Little Girl," she says.

As soon as the family members have dressed and rolled up their bedding, Kaya, Pi-lah-ka, and I walk to the horse herd. Then the three of us ride out to where we left Little Girl, Pi-lah-ka on his stallion and Kaya and I riding double on another horse.

I strain to look as we draw near. There is the little patch of grass, but it's empty. We slide from our horse and search every inch of the clearing. Little Girl is nowhere to be found.

"She's gone!" Kaya cries.

Pi-lah-ka scans the ground. "No broken grass, no sign of a struggle. She might have wandered off."

We mount again and leave the clearing at a walk. My throat aches with the effort of keeping back the tears. "Kaya? Are you all right?" I ask.

Kaya swipes her hand over her cheeks before she

responds. "Maybe we should have stayed with her," she says.

I was thinking the same thing. We're quiet for a minute, swaying with the horse as it walks steadily along the plain. I think of Kaya looking Little Girl deep in her eyes. "I think Little Girl understood that we were doing our best," I finally say. "You told her."

"I did?" Kaya says.

"Remember? Before we left. You told her not to be afraid. She was listening to you, I could tell."

"Was she truly listening?" Kaya asks. She twists around so she can see me.

"I think she was," I say honestly. "You two understood each other."

Kaya squeezes my hand. "*Katsee-yow-yow* for telling me that, my friend."

Then Pi-lah-ka, cresting a small hill in front of us, calls back, "Kaya, there is something that you'll want to see."

◈ *Turn to page 173.*

Kaya picks up the pup and giggles as he licks her face. She strokes his ears, just as I saw her do with Long Legs. My stomach feels like it's on a long roller-coaster drop—one with no end. "Isn't he precious?" Kaya says to me. The puppy gives a little bark, as if he knows Kaya's talking about him.

My mouth is dry, but my palms are wet with sweat. I stare at the puppy, but I don't see him. Instead, all I can see is my only link to home walking away—on the wrist of someone I can't even talk to!

Then Kaya hands the puppy back to the girl and throws her more words. "What did you say?" I ask anxiously.

"I told her that I couldn't trade the bracelet," Kaya tells me. "I said I was sorry, but it's too special. It's from my trading partner."

My muscles go limp with relief. The girl looks disappointed but nods and wanders away, her puppy under her arm. Still, my mind is all rumpled up. The bracelet is on Kaya's wrist—thank goodness—but not mine. Suddenly, I feel that I have to get it back, but I don't want to damage our bond.

A dance is starting nearby—older girls are forming

a circle and the older boys are making another circle around them. "It's the courtship dance," Kaya murmurs. "See, there's Brown Deer." She points to her tall sister, who stands very straight and graceful. "If a boy likes a girl, he tries to dance near her."

The dance starts, and the drums beat an irresistible tempo. The deep thump seems to beat in my chest, like another voice joining the endless roar of the falls. My pulse beats with the drum rhythm, and I long to give myself over to it and practice the dance steps the way Kaya is doing. But I can't stop thinking about my bracelet.

"Here, try this!" Kaya says. "First you step on this foot, and then stomp—" She stops. "What's wrong?"

I look at her miserably. "I—I can't say." I try not to let tears trickle down my face. I've noticed there's not a whole lot of crying going on among *Nimíipuu*.

Kaya looks closely at my face and then lays her hand on my arm. The bracelet's shell gleams like a pearl against her tan skin. "Let's go back to the tepee. Kautsa is there."

❖ *Turn to page 167.*

I take a deep breath and tell myself to be strong.

If Kaya is truly my friend, she'll understand my attachment to the bracelet.

"Kaya, I can't trade my bracelet. It's my connection to my family." I feel a twist in my stomach as I think of Mom and Dad. I miss them. "I don't have anything to trade for your necklace, so I can't keep it." I hold Kaya's necklace back out to her. "I can't be your trading partner," I say sadly.

"Don't be foolish!" Kaya cries. "We can still be trading partners. This will just be a gift." She takes the necklace from my hand and starts to tie it around my neck.

"Wait!" I say. I reach up and untie the bone-bead necklace I wove earlier. "Here! It's not the bracelet, but will you accept this in trade?"

"Of course I will!" Kaya says.

As we tie the necklaces around each other's necks, I'm grateful that Kaya understood why I couldn't give her my bracelet. And I'm glad I was honest with her—even if it took some courage to speak up.

※ *Turn to page 181.*

Down by the riverbank, I kneel behind a canoe, thankful for the deep shadows that hide me from people passing nearby. I take a deep breath and place my fingertip on the edge of the shell. I squeeze my eyes shut and trace a circle around its edge.

Immediately, the rough wood of the canoe against my knees and the dirt under my legs disappear into black space. At the same time, the whirling begins, twirling me around and around until I land with a *thunk* on soft carpet.

I open my eyes. I'm lying on the floor in my bedroom. I'm wearing my PJ's and slippers, and the phone is still ringing in Mom's study. I push myself upright, shaking my head. I'm back, safe. There are no raiders here, I think as I look around the cozy room. I breathe a sigh of relief.

But as I climb into my bed between soft sheets, sadness grips me all of a sudden. There's no Kaya. My friend's round face and sparkling eyes seem so far away. Did I really know her? Did I really ride a horse and run from enemy raiders? Did I spend a day outside enjoying how beautiful nature can be beyond my tidy garden?

I picture Kaya's strong figure standing at the top of the riverbank. *I've carried some of her bravery back with me*, I tell myself. I hoist myself onto my stomach and reach for my cell phone on my bedside table. I thumb through my numbers until I find the one I'm looking for. "Hello, Lily?" I say when my best friend answers. "About that camp . . ."

❖ *The End* ❖

To read this story another way and see how different choices lead to a different ending, turn back to page 84.

Kautsa is sitting inside the tepee when we return. Wing Feather and Sparrow sleep nearby under their rabbit-skin blankets.

"You've returned from the festivities so soon, girls," Kautsa says.

"We felt like resting," Kaya says, glancing at me.

I nod, not trusting my voice. Kautsa glances from me to Kaya. She seems to be waiting for one of us to say something more.

"Then sit here. I made some willow-bark tea." She pours each of us a horn cup of the fragrant brew. The steam bathes my face, and I inhale the delicate aroma. Kautsa settles herself near us and takes up the bag she was weaving when we came in. "I sense that your spirit is troubled, New Friend." Her fingers move gently along the fibers. "What is bothering you?"

I look up at her finely wrinkled face and then at Kaya's worried eyes across the fire. There's a block inside me that won't let me speak, even though I want to. It's just like when Ms. Wallace asked me if I wanted to talk about the garden mess at home.

Kautsa must read something in my face, because she says, "Kaya, the fire is low. We need more wood."

Kaya jumps up right away. "I'll get some." She lifts the flap of the tepee and disappears outside.

Kautsa puts her hand over mine. "Tell me your thoughts. Have you and Kaya had trouble together?"

I look down at our two hands—one smooth, the other wrinkled. Kaya loves and respects Kautsa so much. She always listens to her advice. I desperately need some right now.

Haltingly, I explain the trade Kaya and I made. "I'm worried that Kaya won't want my friendship if I ask for the bracelet back."

Kautsa listens silently until I'm finished. Then she holds up the bag she had been weaving and fingers the threads. "Friends are like fibers woven together. Once they are entwined, they are hard to pick apart. You and Kaya have knit yourselves together. A small thing like this cannot pull you apart so easily." She smiles, and her eyes crinkle at the corners. "Talk to your friend. I think you will be surprised at what she says."

※ *Turn to page 172.*

Kaya and I sit for what feels like hours, waiting for Toe-ta to return. We are surrounded by her family, and homesickness sweeps over me again and again. The silken thread thrown out over the years is pulling me gently back. But I cannot leave until I know that Kaya's father and uncle are safe.

Just when I don't think I can bear the waiting any longer, Long Legs begins to bark. Soon we hear footsteps.

"Two people are approaching," Speaking Rain says. Her voice holds the hope we all have.

Two figures appear out of the shadows. "Toe-ta!" Kaya cries. "Jumps Back! You are safe!"

There's a flurry of voices tumbling over one another as everyone welcomes the men back. Eetsa and Brown Deer hurry to fill bowls with fish soup, and Toe-ta and Jumps Back explain how they got the horses back from the raiders. "We are all safe," Toe-ta says. He turns to Kaya and me. "I am glad you two are safe," he adds. "That has been my worry since we were separated."

When the soup and stories are finished, I know that it's my turn to say good-bye. "Kaya, it's time for me to go back to my family." I look into my friend's face and

recall Bear Blanket's words. "The healer was right.
I have found what I need here. It's time for my journey
to continue."

Kaya and her family rise from their mats. I feel such
gratitude for each of them. "Thank you for helping me
and caring for me," I say.

"Good crossing, young one," Kautsa says. The
kindness and strength of her smile go straight to my
heart.

Kaya walks me down to the edge of the river and
asks a fisherman to take me across in his canoe. "Don't
forget your breathing," I tell Kaya. "You're more patient
than you think."

"I won't forget. I won't forget *you*, New Friend."
She smiles, but her voice has a catch in it. "And you'll
remember how strong you were with our horse
training."

All I can do is nod and squeeze Kaya's hand
because I'm too overcome with emotion to speak.
I climb into the canoe and sit, twisting around to wave
at Kaya as the water separating us grows wider and
wider. She's only a little brown dot when I reach the
opposite shore and hurry behind a small tree.

I take one last look around, then rest my fingertips on the edge of the shell in my bracelet, and once more, trace a circle around the outside.

❊❖ *Turn to page 178.*

Kaya comes back and feeds the fire with the wood she's brought. I look at her familiar face across the flames. Kautsa is right. Kaya is my true friend.

"Kaya, I have to tell you something," I say. My voice wavers a little.

Her brow creases. "I knew something was wrong. What troubles you?"

I meet Kaya's gaze. "I shouldn't have traded you my bracelet. I'm sorry. It's just too special to me. It reminds me of home, even though I've been confused about where home is." I untie her necklace and hold it out. "Can we trade back?"

"Of course we can!" she says immediately. She picks at the knot tying the bracelet to her wrist. "This would have reminded me of our friendship, but I can't ever forget you, even if I don't have the bracelet."

She slips the bracelet back onto my wrist. I have to stop myself from kissing it in relief.

I take a deep breath. "There's something else I have to tell you."

◈ *Turn to page 176.*

Kaya urges our horse forward. At the top of the hill we see Kaya's father. He's mounted on his big stallion, and he's slowly leading Little Girl!

"Toe-ta! I'm so glad you're safe!" Kaya cries as she slides off the horse we're riding.

"*Aa-heh*, the herd is safe too," Toe-ta answers. "Jumps Back and the others are bringing the rest of the horses in."

"Where did you find Little Girl?" Kaya asks, stroking the young horse's nose.

"In the clearing," Toe-ta says.

Kaya looks puzzled. "But we were just in the clearing, looking for her."

"I took her to the stream for water," Toe-ta explains, climbing off his horse. "Her wound is better after resting. You were wise to leave her here. She will need good care back at camp. Will you help her?"

"Oh, yes, Toe-ta!" Kaya answers eagerly.

Back at camp, Kaya and I rub the filly with a soft piece of buckskin and pull burrs and twigs from her coat. "Don't worry, little one," Kaya croons to her.

"You're safe now." She runs her hands under the filly's mane, and the horse arches her neck at Kaya's touch. "I think I will call her Steps High," Kaya says. "That's what she'll do once her leg is better."

I grin. "She'll 'step high' once more—that's wonderful!"

I smile, watching the two of them together. A little twinge tugs at me. Now that we're all safe, I know I need to go home. I touch Steps High's nose, soft as velvet. "Kaya . . ." I say and stop. The words are stuck in my throat.

But she can tell. "It's time for you to move on now, isn't it?" she asks. She tries to smile, but I can see the sadness clouding her face.

I can only nod. Suddenly I feel how much I'll miss Kaya.

"Have you found what you were searching for?" Kaya asks.

I think about how Kaya's people live so closely with the earth and the animals. I've known that feeling of connection. I get it when I dig in my garden, touching the dirt and the seedlings and watching them soak up the water I give them. Now I realize I can enjoy the outdoors while trying other adventures. It took a visit to Kaya's world to help me realize that.

"Yes," I say. "I think I have. I'm never going to forget you, Kaya. Or you, Steps High," I say to Kaya's horse.

Kaya meets my eyes. "I won't forget you," she says. "You have met many challenges already. I think you will meet whatever lies ahead with great strength."

"*Katsee-yow-yow,*" I say to my friend. Then I squeeze Kaya's hand and walk away down the path toward the river—and home.

◈ *The End* ◈

To read this story another way and see how different choices lead to a different ending, turn back to page 110.

You can tell me anything," Kaya says.

"It's time for me to go home," I tell her. "I'm grateful for your help today, and I'm never, ever going to forget all that I learned from you."

Kaya's eyes are bright with friendship. I reach out and squeeze her hand. Then I look at Kautsa's wise face. I want to give her something, to thank her for taking care of me and helping me so much. But I don't have anything to give. That's when I remember the pink stone I found when I was out with Kaya. I take it out of the pouch at my waist and hand it to Kautsa. "Will you take this gift? I want to thank you for the wisdom you've shared with me." I try to speak as respectfully as Kaya does.

Kautsa takes the stone and turns it over in her hands. *"Katsee-yow-yow.* I am glad you spoke what was in your heart. You are quiet but strong—like this stone."

Before today, I didn't think of myself as strong. But maybe Kautsa is right. I know I've become stronger here in Kaya's world.

"I'll go with you to the river." Kaya starts to get up, but Kautsa puts out her hand.

"I think our friend is ready to make her own way home." Her piercing eyes move over my face, and a little shiver runs down my back. Kautsa really does think I'm strong. She believes I can take the next steps of my journey on my own.

I slip out of the tepee and down the path. Hidden safely from view, I trace the shell in the bracelet.

❖ *Turn to page 180.*

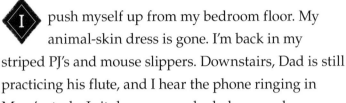 push myself up from my bedroom floor. My animal-skin dress is gone. I'm back in my striped PJ's and mouse slippers. Downstairs, Dad is still practicing his flute, and I hear the phone ringing in Mom's study. I sit down on my bed, draw my knees up under my chin, and wrap my arms around my legs. I still have the bracelet, and the sore muscles from my day with Kaya. Did I really ride with her out on the grasslands? Did I really feel the warm, damp hair of the horses and look into their big dark eyes? It all feels so far away, sitting here, enclosed by four walls with air-conditioning flowing from the vents and electric lights overhead. Kaya's face swims up in front of me. She was so at home in the wide-open outdoors.

Suddenly, I jump up. I fling open my bedroom door, pound down the stairs to the living room, and wrap my arms around Dad, almost knocking him over.

"Whoa, Wheels. Everything all right?" He hugs me back, his flute in one hand. Mom comes out of her study.

"What's wrong?" She hurries over to us, and I disentangle one arm from Dad and wrap it around her,

so now I'm hugging them both.

"Nothing," I say, my face still buried in the front of Dad's shirt. "I'm just glad to be home."

Mom drops a kiss on top of my head. "You must have fallen asleep up in your room and journeyed far away in your dreams."

"Yeah . . ." I smile to myself. "Something like that."

Dad picks up his flute again, and I stroll to the screen door and open it, wandering over the cool grass to my garden. I step over the little picket fence and fall to my knees in the soft dirt. The neat rows of peppers, carrots, and tomatoes stretch before me, silvery in the light of the rising moon. This is where Kaya would want to be, if she came to my world. And this is where I can remember her best. Outside. Close to nature.

◈ *The End* ◈

To read this story another way and see how different choices lead to a different ending, turn back to page 68.

I'm back in my own bedroom, wearing my pajamas and my mouse slippers. I'm limp with relief at being back, but as I climb onto my bed and fall back against the pillows, my heart is heavy. I've traded one world for the other. Although I'm glad to be home, I miss Kaya.

As I settle into the darkening room, I realize that I didn't leave her behind entirely. I brought back everything I learned from her: trusting elders, taking care of one another, respecting the earth. I can do all of those things here at home—and at school.

The next day, I hurry to catch up to Ms. Wallace as everyone leaves the classroom for the short walk to the garden. "Could I talk to you for a minute?" I ask with the courage I learned from Kaya.

"Of course!" she says right away. Her brown eyes remind me of Kautsa's: wise and kind and ready to help. I take a deep breath. "I need some advice. About my group . . ."

◈ *The End* ◈

To read this story another way and see how different choices lead to a different ending, turn back to page 52.

As Kaya and I wander toward the irresistible beat of the drums, I think about home. I touch the bracelet on my wrist. It's time to go soon. But as we get close to the drums, the pulse of the beat puts thoughts of home out of my mind for a moment.

Kaya seizes my hand and pulls me toward a group of girls dancing in a rough circle on the grass. They step forward, then back, stamping their feet, making the fringe on their dresses snap with each step.

I try to hang back. "I don't think I can remember this dance tonight."

"I'll help you!" Kaya pulls me forward into the circle. Hesitantly, I try to follow Kaya's feet as they step and stamp.

"That's it!" Kaya encourages me.

I look down at my moccasins. They're moving at the same time as Kaya's. A little burst of pride goes through me, and I look around the circle and smile. The drums carry me along with their beat. It's so much like the Wallowa pow-wow from last summer that I can't help thinking I see myself and Mom and Dad standing in the crowd of people watching. All that's missing are the lawn chairs and horse trailers.

The girls who dance in the modern pow-wow wear colorful dresses decorated with many more beads than Kaya and her friends are wearing now. They arrive at the celebrations in cars and trucks instead of on horseback. But all these girls share a history and traditions that I've discovered during my time with Kaya.

As we dance together, I think Kaya would be pleased to know that her people—and their dances—are still alive today.

❖ *The End* ❖

To read this story another way and see how different choices lead to a different ending, turn back to page 152.

ABOUT Kaya's Time

Like all *Nimíipuu* children, Kaya grew up under the watchful eyes of a large, loving family. Grandparents were a child's main teachers, and brothers, sisters, and cousins all learned and played together and looked after one another. Young children spent lots of time outdoors exploring the world around them. Handmade toys and games kept them entertained while others worked, and helped them learn the skills they'd need later in life. Stick horses gave children practice in caring for horses—and the chance to imagine themselves as warrior men and women.

When Kaya's grandmother was a girl, horses were not part of *Nimíipuu* life. But children like Kaya grew up with horses. By the time they were nine or ten, children rode well, and they knew how to train and care for their horses.

Nimíipuu girls and boys were taught to respect all creatures with whom they shared the land. Each day, Kaya began her day with a prayer of thanks to *Hun-ya-wat*, the Creator, for all the living things around her as well as the earth, the sky, and the water. Kaya's people believed that their spirits were part of the land—a land of rugged peaks and deep canyons, dense forests and vast grasslands, gently rolling hills and swift-moving rivers. For thousands of years, Kaya's people had taken care of the land, and it had given them everything they needed to survive and grow strong.

The seasons brought change and the opportunity to travel, which *Nimíipuu* loved to do. Kaya and her family followed the seasons to gather roots and berries and to hunt and fish. In early spring, when salmon reached the canyon streams, the *Nimíipuu* traveled to the traditional fishing grounds at Celilo Falls. Kaya's people joined thousands of other Indian people to celebrate the return of the salmon and to fish the wild waters at the base of the thunderous falls.

Salmon season at Celilo was the most festive time of year. Everyone enjoyed the feasting and dancing. At night, the drumming would begin. Dancers moved with dignity and grace, heads held high and backs kept straight, while they gently stepped to the beat of the drums. There were also games, races, and trading to enjoy. For thousands of years, Celilo Falls was one of the greatest trading sites on the whole continent. People came from as far away as modern-day California, Alaska, and Missouri to trade everything from blankets to buffalo robes, horses to hand-painted hides. People from different tribes often became lifelong trading partners and friends.

Today, one of the most exciting and beautiful celebrations of Indian culture is the modern pow-wow. *Nimíipuu*, known now as the *Nez Perce*, gather to celebrate their heritage. They camp, reunite with family and friends, listen to the drumming, and dance.

GLOSSARY of Nez Perce Words

In the story, Nez Perce words are spelled so that English readers can pronounce them. Here, you can also see how the words are actually spelled and said by the Nez Perce people.

PHONETIC/ NEZ PERCE	PRONUNCIATION	MEANING
aa-heh/´éehe	*AA-heh*	yes, that's right
Eetsa/Iice	*EET-sah*	mother
Hun-ya-wat/ Hanyaw´áat	*hun-yah-WAHT*	the Creator
katsee-yow-yow/ qe´ci´yew´yew´	*KAHT-see-yow-yow*	thank you
Kautsa/Qáaca´c	KOUT-sah	grandmother from mother's side
Kaya´aton´my´	*ky-YAAH-a-ton-my*	she who arranges rocks
Nimíipuu	*nee-MEE-poo*	The People; known today as the Nez Perce

Pi-lah-ka/Piláqá .... *pee-LAH-kah*.................grandfather from
mother's side

tawts/ta´c................*TAWTS*.......................good

**tawts may-we/
ta´c méeywi**.............*TAWTS MAY-wee*...........good morning

Toe-ta/Toot´a..........*TOH-tah*......................father

**Wallowa/
Wal´áwa**...................*wah-LAU-wa*..................Wallowa Valley
in present-day
Oregon

Read more of KAYA'S stories,
available from booksellers and at *americangirl.com*

❈ *Classics* ❈
Kaya's classic series, now in two volumes:

Volume 1:
The Journey Begins
When Kaya and her blind sister are captured by an enemy tribe, it takes all of her courage and skill to survive. If she escapes, will she ever see her sister— and her Appaloosa mare, Steps High—again?

Volume 2:
Smoke on the Wind
Kaya's pup, Tatlo, gives her comfort while she searches for her lost sister and her beloved horse, Steps High. When a forest fire threatens all she holds dear, Kaya must face her greatest fear yet.

❈ *Journey in Time* ❈
Travel back in time—and spend a day with Kaya!

The Roar of the Falls
What's it like to live in Kaya's world? Ride bareback, sleep in a tepee, and help Kaya train a filly—but watch out for bears! Choose your own path through this multiple-ending story.

❈ *Mystery* ❈
Another thrilling adventure with Kaya!

The Silent Stranger
During the winter spirit dances, a strange woman appears in Kaya's village. Why is she alone, and why will she not speak? To find out the truth, Kaya must look deep into her own heart.

❈ *A Sneak Peek at* ❈

The Journey Begins

A Kaya Classic

Volume 1

What happens to Kaya?
Find out in the first volume of her classic stories.

isten!" Kautsa said in a low voice. "The dogs are growling! Wake up!"

Kaya tried to waken in the deep of night. She heard Kautsa's sharp command, but sleep was like a hand pushing her down. Nearby, some dogs growled, then began to bark fiercely. Kaya sat up and rubbed her eyes. What was wrong?

Her mother peeked out the door of the dark tepee, then ducked back inside. "Strangers in our camp!" Eetsa said. "Get dressed! Quick! Enemies!"

Enemies! Enemies in their camp! The warning was a jolt of lightning—swiftly Kaya was on her feet. Her heart pounding, she struggled into her dress. Kautsa, Brown Deer, and Speaking Rain were doing the same. They all tugged on their moccasins and crept out of the tepee. Kautsa pushed Speaking Rain and the twin boys ahead of her. Brown Deer picked up one of the little boys. Eetsa picked up the other one. "Follow me!" Eetsa whispered. "Kaya, take Speaking Rain to the woods! We'll hide there!" Crouching, Eetsa ran for the trees, Brown Deer and Kautsa right on her heels.

The moon was rising above the trees bordering the clearing. Kaya could see women, children, and

old people hurrying from the tepees for safety in
the woods. Some men ran toward the edge of the
camp where dark figures ducked between the horses
tethered there. Raiders! Enemy raiders! They'd slipped
into camp hoping to make off with the best horses,
but the dogs had given them away.

Kaya's mouth was dry with alarm. She clasped
Speaking Rain's hand tightly. But instead of following
Eetsa into the woods, as she'd been told, she went in
the direction of the herd. Where was Steps High?
Would raiders try to steal her horse?

Kaya saw the woman named Swan Circling head
toward the horses, too. A raider was about to cut the
rawhide line that tethered her fine horse. Swan Circling
had as much courage as any warrior. She stabbed at the
raider with her digging stick. She knocked him away
from her horse, which reared and whinnied in panic.

The raider leaped onto the back of another horse
he'd already cut loose. With a fierce cry, he swung the
horse around and galloped straight through camp,
coming right at Kaya and Speaking Rain!

With a gasp of fear, Kaya tried to run out of his
way, pulling Speaking Rain behind her. Too late! Kaya

threw herself onto her stomach, dragging Speaking Rain down with her. The raider jumped his horse over them and plunged on.

Kaya struggled to her knees. Now other raiders raced through the camp toward the herd. They lay low on their horses, trying to stampede the herd so no one could ride after them. The horses snorted and screamed with alarm. A few broke away. Was Steps High with them? Kaya whirled around. *Nimíipuu* men with bows and arrows were running to cut off the raiders.

Arrows hissed by. Kaya clasped Speaking Rain's hand again and ran for the safety of the woods. A horse brushed against her, almost knocking her down. She felt someone seize her hair, then grasp her arm. Speaking Rain's hand was yanked from hers. A raider swung Kaya roughly behind him onto his horse. She sank her teeth into his arm, but he broke her hold with a slap.

Kaya looked back for Speaking Rain. Another raider was dragging her onto his horse. "Speaking Rain!" Kaya cried. The raiders raced after the herd, which ran full out now. The *Nimíipuu* men gave chase on foot, but they were quickly outdistanced.

Terrified, Kaya clung to the raider's back. The herd was thundering down the valley, the raiders in the rear. The night was filled with boiling dust. Hoofbeats shook the ground and echoed in Kaya's chest. She caught a glimpse of Steps High running with the others. Her horse had been stolen by the enemies. She was their captive, too, and so was Speaking Rain. And it was Kaya's fault!

All that night, and on through the next day and night, the raiders ran the stolen horses eastward. When their mounts tired, they paused only briefly before jumping onto fresh horses and going on. Kaya knew they wanted to get out of *Nimíipuu* country before they were caught.

Because the raiders didn't rest, Kaya and Speaking Rain couldn't rest, either. The mountains and the valleys below went by in a blur. In her fatigue, Kaya sometimes thought she saw a blue lake in the sky. Sometimes she thought the distant, rolling hills were huge buffalo. And sometimes she did fall asleep, her head bumping the raider's back. He slapped her legs to waken her. She thought, then, about jumping off the running horse, but she knew she'd be injured or killed on the narrow, stony trail. *Maybe it would be better to die than to be a captive,* Kaya thought. But she couldn't abandon Speaking Rain.

When the sun was high overhead, the raiders finally stopped to rest. They left a scout to guard their trail and took the herd to a grassy spot by a little lake where the horses could feed and drink. Kaya saw Steps High standing by the water with the other foam-flecked horses. Their heads were down and their chests heaved from the punishing journey. How she wished she could go to her horse!

When the raiders gathered to share dried meat, Kaya got a better look at them. They were young, bold, and proud of themselves for stealing so many fine horses. She thought they spoke the language of enemies from Buffalo Country. Though Kaya couldn't understand their words, she knew that they boasted of their success. Perhaps they were proud, too, that they had driven the herd all the way through *Nimíipuu* country to the northern trail through the Bitterroot Mountains.

The raider who'd seized Speaking Rain offered her some of the buffalo meat. When she didn't respond, he

waved his hand in front of her eyes, then made a noise
of disgust. Kaya knew he was angry that the girl he'd
captured for a slave was blind. He pushed her down
beside Kaya and stalked back to the circle of men.
Kaya held her close.

Speaking Rain leaned against Kaya's shoulder.
"Where are we?" she whispered.

"Somewhere on the trail to Buffalo Country," Kaya
whispered back. She put some of the food she'd been
given into Speaking Rain's hand.

"What will happen to us?" Speaking Rain's voice
quavered.

Though Kaya trembled with fatigue, she kept her
voice steady. "Don't you remember what happened
when enemies from the south stole some of our horses?
Our father and the other warriors got ready for a raid.
As the drummers beat the drums, all the women sang
songs to send off our warriors with courage. Our
warriors followed the enemies over the mountains
and brought back all our horses! Our warriors will
make a raid on these men, too. They'll take you and
me back home with them. And they'll take back all of
our horses, as well."

"Are you sure?" Speaking Rain murmured.

"*Aa-heh!*" Kaya whispered. "I'm sure."

But, in her heart, Kaya was far from certain. They'd traveled a long way over the mountains already. Toe-ta and the other men might not have returned to the berry-picking camp yet. When they did, the raiders might have already left the mountains and hidden themselves securely in the country to the east. What would happen to Kaya and Speaking Rain—and Steps High—then?

About the Author

First, EMMA CARLSON BERNE
thought she was going to be a college
professor, so she went to graduate school
at Miami University in Ohio. After that,
she taught horseback riding in Boston and
Charleston, South Carolina. *Then* Emma
found out how much she enjoys writing
for children and young adults.
Since that time, Emma has authored over
two dozen books and often writes about
historical figures such as Sacagawea,
Helen Keller, Christopher Columbus, and
the artist Frida Kahlo. Emma lives in a
hundred-year-old house in Cincinnati, Ohio,
with her two little boys and her husband.
She loves to walk in the woods and pick
berries, just like Kaya.